Lily and the Creep

Other Books Available

The Lily Series
   Here's Lily!
   Lily Robbins, M.D. (Medical Dabbler)
   Lily and the Creep
   Lily's Ultimate Party
   Ask Lily
   Lily the Rebel
   Lights, Action, Lily!
   Lily Rules!
   Rough & Rugged Lily
   Lily Speaks!
   Horse Crazy Lily
   Lily's Church Camp Adventure
   Lily's Passport to Paris
   Lily's in London?!

Nonfiction
   The Beauty Book
   The Body Book
   The Buddy Book
   The Best Bash Book
   The Blurry Rules Book
   The It's MY Life Book
   The Creativity Book
   The Uniquely Me Book
   The Year 'Round Holiday Book
   The Values & Virtues Book
   The Fun-Finder Book
   The Walk-the-Walk Book
   Dear Diary
   Girlz Want to Know
   NIV Young Women of Faith Bible
   Take It from Me

Lily and the Creep

Nancy Rue

zonderkidz

We want to hear from you. Please send your comments about this book to us in care of the address below. Thank you.

zonder**kidz**

Grand Rapids, MI 49530
www.zonderkidz.com

The children's group of Zondervan

Lily and the Creep
Copyright © 2001 by Women of Faith

Requests for information should be addressed to:
Zonderkidz, *Grand Rapids, Michigan 49530*
www.zonderkidz.com

ISBN-10: 0-310-23252-X
ISBN-13: 978-0-310-23252-0

Published in association with the literary agency of Alive Communications, Inc., 7680 Goddard Street, Suite 200, Colorado Springs, CO 80920.

Art direction and interior design by Amy Langeler

Printed in the United States of America

06 07 08 09 • 24 23 22 21 20

Chapter 1

"Hey, Robbins," Leo Cooks hissed in Lily's ear.

Don't answer, Lily Robbins told herself sternly. *It's a trick.*

She concentrated on not touching his sweaty hand—even though Ms. Gooch had said "join hands with your partner."

"Ms. Gooch is lookin' at ya," Leo whispered.

His breath was hot, and it made Lily want to slap her hand over her ear, but she ignored him.

"She's givin' you the eyebrow," Leo persisted.

That was not a good thing. The teacher's eyebrow was usually the last warning sign before a name went on the board or something. *Don't fall into this absurd little creep's trap,* Lily thought.

Leo wasn't actually little. He was even bigger than his buddy Shad Shifferdecker, who was at this very moment managing to step all over the feet of his partner—Lily's best friend, Reni Johnson. Even as Lily watched, he caught Reni on the side of her Nike with his left Timberland. She jabbed him in the ribs with her elbow.

Don't let him know he's getting to you, Reni, Lily thought.

Right. Just then Leo jabbed *her* in the side and hissed, "You better take my hand. Ms. Gooch's got both eyebrows goin'!"

Both eyebrows *and* the don't-start-with-me tone. "Join *hands,* people," she called out over the blaring of Italian music.

Taking a breath full of dread, Lily slid her hand into Leo's. He squeezed it like he was wringing out a dishrag, and suddenly, Lily felt a jolt go up her arm. Before she could stop herself, she'd let out a yell.

The music came to an abrupt halt, and Ms. Gooch planted her hands on her hips. Both black eyebrows were in full gear.

"All right, who's yelling?" she said.

"It was Lily," Marcie McCleary said.

Lily tucked a curl of red hair behind her ear and otherwise tried to look innocent.

"All right, you two," Ms. Gooch said. "What's going on?"

I wasn't doing anything! Lily wanted to protest. *It was him!*

Still, Lily pressed her full lips together and kept quiet. She'd die before she'd be a tattletale like Marcie McCleary.

"So what's the story?" Ms. Gooch said.

"I don't know," Leo said. "You told us to join hands, so I grabbed hers and she started yelling."

"Is there a problem, Lily?"

"Lily *is* a problem," Shad Shifferdecker said.

Daniel Tibbetts snorted. Ms. Gooch waved both of them off with an impatient hand. She didn't lose patience often, and the class got that uncomfortable kind of quiet like when they were waiting to see if somebody was going to get sent to the office.

"Lily," she said again, "*is* there a problem?"

Lily rubbed her fingers into her palm where moments ago Leo had set off some kind of buzzer-shock thing. But she shook her head no.

"No," she said. "Everything's fine."

"Do you always yell when everything's fine?" Ashley asked.

Ashley's best friend, Chelsea Green, let out her shriek of a laugh, and Marcie joined in because she always joined in when Ashley and Chelsea laughed, whether she knew what they were laughing at or not. Lily noticed with relief that *her* friends continued to glare at Leo and Shad.

"We're about finished here anyway," Ms. Gooch said. "Let's go back to the room."

Leo left Lily's side with a flailing of long arms and legs. Lily did her most poised walk up to the tape recorder where Ms. Gooch was busily pushing buttons.

"Ms. Gooch?" Lily said. "I'm really sorry."

Ms. Gooch frowned down at the tape deck. "I'm sure you were provoked. You want to tell me what was going on?"

"It wasn't that big of a deal. I just overreacted."

Lily could see Ms. Gooch was trying to smother a smile. "'Over-reacted'?" she said.

"Yes," Lily replied. It was a term her mother used all the time when she was talking about the way Lily responded to her two brothers.

"So what were you 'overreacting' *to*?" Ms. Gooch said.

"I don't want to say. Could I change partners?"

"Nope. Sorry," Ms. Gooch said. "If I let you switch, I'll have every-body and her dog up here whining. I ought to just let you girls all dance with each other, but then I'd have to let the boys dance with each other, and we'd have even worse chaos." She shook her head at Lily again. "Just tough it out, Lily," she said. "If anybody can do it, you can."

At any other time, a compliment like that would have had Lily walking out of the multipurpose room with her spirit soaring. But right now, she didn't care how tough she was. She was sick of dealing with Leo and Daniel and, worst of all, Shad. He was the one who had put Leo up to it, that was plain.

"Whoa, she really must have yelled at you," Zooey said as Lily pushed her way through the double doors and out into the courtyard where the Girlz were gathered.

They were all there—the whole Girlz Only Club—Reni and Zooey and Kresha and Suzy. It made Lily feel better already to have them around her—Reni's black face set to get revenge and Zooey's round one flushed with concern, Suzy's tiny eyebrows all puckered up in worry, and Kresha's pale eyes peeking hopefully through her straggly bangs.

"Men," Zooey said in disgust.

"They're the worst," Reni said. "I thought I had it bad having to dance with Shad, but you got it even worse. The whole time I was waiting for him to do something to me, and all the time it was Leo he had doing the dirty work. I shoulda known."

"What do we do?" Zooey said. "I have to dance with Daniel, which means I'm probably next, which means—" Zooey's voice was starting to wind up into a whine.

"Don' vorry about it," Kresha said. Her eyes were crinkling behind her bangs, and she flung a skinny arm around Lily's neck. Kresha was the most touchy-feely of all of them. The Girlz had decided it must be because she was Croatian. They probably did a lot of hugging in Croatia or something.

"Lee-lee will think of something," she said now. "She alvez does."

"Well, you better think of something fast," Reni said, "before I have to smack somebody."

"Would you really hit one of them?" Zooey said, eyes round.

"No, I would not," Reni said. "But I'd sure like to."

"Okay, so I'll think of something," Lily said. "Tomorrow."

"Not today?" Kresha said.

"No—remember today we got to clean the clubhouse," Reni said. "Or my mama says she's gonna close us down."

"It is getting kind of disgusting in there," Lily said.

They met every day after school in the playhouse-turned-clubhouse in Reni's backyard. Reni's mother decreed no more meetings until it was cleaned.

Besides, Lily thought, *it'll give me some time to think of something.*

It was always up to her to come up with solutions to their problems. She didn't mind that—in fact, she kind of liked it. It was time she started looking for a new direction for her life anyway, she decided. It was the never-ending quest . . . trying to figure out who *she* was.

The trouble was, this thing with the boys had been going on all year, and although she'd learned a lot since last fall, she still hadn't figured out how to keep Shad, Leo, and Daniel from constantly messing things up for the Girlz. Looking better, feeling better—those were cool things. But so far, they hadn't cracked the boy problem.

"Hey, Snobbins," Shad Shifferdecker hissed as she passed him on the way to the street.

She didn't answer.

"All right, but don't blame me if you walk all the way home with that big piece of toilet paper stuck to your shoe."

Lily looked down in spite of herself. There was nothing stuck to her shoe.

"Ha-ha—made ya look!" Shad said.

The Girlz were right. She had to think of something before the boys got control of them completely.

Chapter 2

When the Girlz finished cleaning the clubhouse that afternoon, it was five o'clock. The air was still pretty warm though as Lily hurried for home just a few blocks from Reni's. It was finally spring in New Jersey, at least spring enough not to have to bundle up to your eyeballs every time you went out the door. Those first few days without a coat always made Lily feel free, and she put on her backpack so she could swing her arms. She was happily walking along, thinking things really weren't that bad as long as you had puddles and the Girlz Only Group, when she heard fast footsteps behind her.

Lily stepped off the sidewalk and glanced over her shoulder to let whomever it was pass. She was just in time to see Daniel put his hand on her backpack.

"What are you doing?" Lily said. "Let go!"

She tried to turn around, batting her hands at him the whole time, but he had a firm grip.

"No, don't!" Lily cried.

But with a tug of each hand, he pulled the zipper wide open. As the books tumbled out onto the sidewalk and papers flew everywhere, Daniel took off, snorting, and Lily could hear Leo and Shad joining in.

Ignore them, she told herself, her face blazing in blotches. But how could she, she wondered, as she retrieved her math homework from a puddle, when they were always doing stupid stuff?

By the time she got to her house, Lily knew her face was beyond blotchy. She didn't even care that there was an unfamiliar car parked in their driveway, which meant they probably had company. She stormed through the living room and dining room and into the kitchen already spewing out the whole story. She had it pretty well wrapped up when her mother looked up at her from the table and said, "Hi, Lil. Nice to see you too. This is Mrs. Cavanaugh."

"Oh," Lily said. "Sorry."

The woman sitting across from Mom at the table grinned at her from a starting-to-wrinkle face. She had short, salt-and-pepper hair and a smile that seemed to stay there all the time.

"Mrs. Cavanaugh's one of our guidance counselors," Mom said.

"Is Art in trouble?" Lily said.

"No," Mrs. Cavanaugh said. "Your mom and I just work together."

"Oh," Lily said again. She should have figured that out, since Mom taught P.E. at the high school. Besides, her older brother was too much Mr. Big Man on Campus to ever get in trouble. Still, a person could always hope.

"Sounds like you're the one with trouble," Mrs. Cavanaugh said as she waved away the plate of Oreos Mom was offering her.

"Nah, the Shad Shifferdecker story never ends," Mom said. "I keep telling her it won't, either, until the boys realize that girls aren't just soft boys."

Mrs. Cavanaugh laughed, but her eyes were still on Lily.

"You know what that's all about, don't you, Lily?" she said.

Lily turned around and politely shook her head.

"This boy—Shad—only teases you because he likes you."

Lily felt her eyes piercing right into Mrs. Cavanaugh. What kind of a counselor *was* she, anyway?

"No, he does *not*!" Lily said. "He calls me 'Snobbins'!"

"Oh, he doesn't *know* he likes you, and he wouldn't admit it if he *did* know. But he's showing all the signs."

"Gross!" Lily said. "I wish he hated me! I *hate* it when he teases me."

"Really?" Mom said dryly. "We hadn't picked up on that."

"I thought after I took that modeling course and learned about self-esteem, well, no, *God*-esteem, and I was feeling good about stuff, I could just ignore him and his little freak friends. But it isn't working!"

"You're developing a strong positive self-image," Mrs. Cavanaugh said. *Now* she was sounding like a counselor. "But it's not completely intact yet."

"'Self-image'?" Lily said.

She pulled out a chair and sat down. Her mother groaned.

Lily ignored her. She was leaning across the table, her face as close as she could get it to Mrs. Cavanaugh's without overturning the plate of cookies. The smile on Mrs. C's face didn't change as she folded her hands and said, "Self-*esteem* is whether you value yourself as a person."

"No problem there," Mom said.

"Self-*image* is more how you see yourself in your mental mirror."

"I have a mental mirror?" Lily said.

"Sure. We all do. It reflects how we see ourselves in our own minds. Your self-image might be completely different from what other people see in you or even from what really is. Maturing is all about getting your self-image and reality to all line up—and it's about you *liking* that."

"Okay," Lily said.

Mrs. Cavanaugh kept smiling. "If you know who you are and you like who you are, teasing just won't bother you in the first place."

"That's it, then," Lily said with a final nod. "I have to get me one of those positive self-image things. How do I do that?"

"Can I say something here?" Mom said. Her big-as-a-doe's brown eyes were shining, although she still wasn't smiling. Lily's mother never smiled that much with her mouth. It was all in her eyes.

"Sure. Jump in any time," Mrs. Cavanaugh said.

"Lil," Mom said, "there is no class you can take to get a self-image, and you can't make it into a career, okay? Are we clear?"

"I *know*, Mom," Lily said, and then whipped her head back toward Mrs. Cavanaugh. "But how *do* I get one?"

"A good self-image comes from really getting to know yourself. It comes gradually as you get to know and like who you really are and weed out all the false stuff." She reached over and patted Lily's hand. "Don't worry. It will happen. You're on your way."

"Yeah, but how can I make it happen faster?"

"Here we go," Mom said. "You don't know our Lil. She goes after things 150 percent. She'll want to read every book on the subject."

"There are books?" Lily said. Her mind was already circling excitedly around the idea of going to the library.

"Well, there *are* some very good books," Mrs. Cavanaugh said.

"No, you may not order them on the Internet," Mom said to Lily.

"Can you write the names down for me?" Lily said.

"I think I have a couple of them in my office at school," Mrs. Cavanaugh said. "You can borrow them. I don't have that many requests for them from the kids I see, trust me. If I did, maybe there wouldn't be so many problems." She gave Lily's hand a squeeze. "I'll send them home with your mom."

"When?" Lily said.

"Lighten up, Lil," Mom said.

Mrs. Cavanaugh's smile came back, and she laughed her face into lines. "I'll send them home tomorrow," she said.

Tomorrow meant when her mom got home from school, Lily knew, and that was too late for the Girlz Only Group meeting. She was going to have to take action sooner, which, of course, she did. That night right after dinner, she talked her dad into taking her to the library at the college.

It wasn't that hard to do. Lily's father was an English professor at the university, and he loved it when any of the three kids showed an interest in hanging out over there. Mostly, that meant Lily.

Lily's little brother, Joe, set foot on campus only when there was a football or basketball game, or maybe a wrestling match, and usually it was Mom who took him to those. And her older brother, Art, could be persuaded to go to concerts, if they were jazz and if he might get to go backstage and hold somebody's saxophone or something.

That was the thing. Everybody in the Robbins family had something they were known for.

Except me, Lily thought, as she hurried down the stairs with her notebook in hand to meet Dad. *I have to find my thing—and I betcha once I get to know myself better, I'll figure it out.*

It wasn't that she hadn't tried already. In the fall, she'd gone to modeling school, but even though she'd been good at it, the Girlz Only Group had won out over that. And in the winter, she'd thought it was medicine that was her future, but she'd learned it would be years before she could actually practice, and she needed an identity right now—before she turned out to be somebody boring.

Somebody Shad Shifferdecker could get away with teasing forever.

"You sure like to rack up brownie points with Dad, don't you?" Art said to her as she was hanging out by the front door, waiting for Dad to find his glasses.

"No," Lily said, wrinkling her nose at her tall, brown-eyed brother. "I have to do some research."

"You could get on the Internet," he said. "You're just trying to impress Dad—which I can understand—I mean, you *would* have to make the effort. I, on the other hand, just naturally blow him away."

He patted Lily on the top of the head. She batted his hand away and went for his short-cropped, reddish-brown curls but missed. He was getting too tall for her to reach and too fast. He was halfway up the stairs before she could start wailing, so she didn't bother.

"Ready, Lilliputian?" Dad said from the doorway, glasses in hand.

"Why do there have to be boys?" Lily said.

Dad blinked his blue Lily-like eyes and brought them into intense focus. "Well," he said, "if there were no boys, there would eventually be no more girls." He frowned. "How far do you want to go with this?"

"Never mind, Daddy," Lily said. "Can we just go to the library?"

Lily's father was one male she liked to be around, and they put their wildly curly red heads together and chatted in whispers in the library. They soon found a stack of books on the subject of self-image it took the two of them to carry. Some of them had hard words in the titles, but Dad said he would help her with anything she didn't understand.

She could barely keep from dragging some of them into Friendly's with her when they stopped for ice cream on the way home, but she didn't want to hurt his feelings by having her nose in a book while he was telling her about some poet, especially while they ate their ice cream walking along the Delaware River. There was a park there and a walkway along the wall that bordered the river. The Delaware was its prettiest at night when you couldn't see how dirty it was.

"The Bard was into self-image," Dad was saying as they reached the wall and started their stroll.

"Who's the Bard?" Lily said.

"That's a nickname for Shakespeare."

"Dad, I don't think they had self-image back then."

"They didn't have the name for it, but they had it. 'To thine own self be true, and it must follow, as the night the day, thou canst not then be false to any man.'"

Dad's blue eyes got that dreamy, faraway look they always took on when he was quoting. Lily tried to tug him back before he put his whole hand in his banana split or something.

"I'm trying to figure out who my own self *is*," she said. "I don't think the Barf can help me with that."

"Bard," Dad said. "Now, if help is what you're looking for, Jesus is your man."

"I *know* they didn't talk about self-image back in *those* days."

"Jesus did." Dad squinted for a moment at the chocolate sauce dripping from his spoon and then said, "Let me see if I can put it into simple terms—let's see, it's Matthew 10 somewhere . . . Jesus said that if your first concern is to look out for yourself, you'll never find yourself. But if you forget about yourself and look at Him, you'll find both yourself *and* Him."

He looked at Lily as if that were supposed to clear up everything. Lily shook her head. "That's not the way Mrs. Cavanaugh explained it."

"Who's Mrs. Cavanaugh?" he said, and then erased his question with his hand. "That isn't the way all those books are going to explain it, either. That's why I want you to promise me something."

"What?" Lily said.

"Promise me that you'll read about self-image in the Bible too. I'll make a list of verses for you. Every time you read from one of your books, I want you to read at least one of the verses from the list."

"Okay," Lily said. Then she couldn't hold it back any longer. "Could we eat the rest of this in the car? I really want to get home and start reading."

"I knew it," Mom said when they walked in the front door with Lily's stacks.

While Dad and Mom had one of those conversations without words that they sometimes had over the kids' heads, Lily went up to her room with as many volumes as she could carry, and lying tummy down on the bed, she dug right into one.

The very first page of the first book had her sitting straight up.

"The first step in developing a positive self-image," it said, "is to stop letting other people determine how you will behave. That's the biggest roadblock to finding your true self."

I know what that means, Lily thought. *We've got to stay as far away from Shad and those guys as we can. We'll start tomorrow.*

And as far as she was concerned, tomorrow couldn't come fast enough.

Chapter 3

It was first recess the next day before Lily even had a chance to tell the Girlz what she'd decided. They gathered under their tree, as far away as possible from the basketball court where Shad and Daniel and Leo were showing off for each other.

"They're doing a lot of damage to our self-images, those boys," Lily told the Girlz. "We have to shut them out of our lives."

Only Kresha looked doubtful. She was twisting a strand of her on-the-brown-side-of-blond hair and looking down at the toe of her dingy sneaker.

"What's wrong?" Lily said.

Kresha smiled, which she usually did. Lily had figured out it was to cover up the fact that some of the time she didn't know what in the world people were talking about. Her English still wasn't that good.

"Do we have to shut up *all* the boys?" Kresha said finally.

"Not shut up, shut out," Lily said patiently.

"I'd like to shut them up," Reni said.

Suzy giggled.

"Vhat does dat mean, Lee-lee?" Kresha said.

"We don't talk to them—we don't look at them—we just pretend they don't exist. That way they can't mess up us trying to find our true selves."

"Vhat is dat—true self?"

"That's what we're trying to find out," Reni said, not so patiently. Her brown eyes flashed. "And we can't do it with those boys breathing down our necks all the time."

"Oh," Kresha said. She crossed her long, lanky arms across her chest and grinned at them. "I *like* boys on my neck."

"No, you do not!" Reni said.

"She didn't mean it like that," Suzy said. But she cocked her silky head at Kresha. "You didn't, did you?"

"I like the boys," Kresha said. She pointed at the knot Shad and Daniel and Leo formed up against the wall of the school. "Those boys sometimes are villains, but some other boys I like."

"Villains?" Zooey said, her little bow mouth hanging open slightly.

"Well, look at them," Reni said. "Look at how they're doin' poor little ol' Yale over there."

All eyes went to the basketball court, where very thin Yale Phillips was standing at the edge of it, trying to dig a hole in the concrete with the toe of his shoe.

"He must've said something dumb again," Zooey said.

"Zooey!" Suzy said.

"Well, every time he says something to them, like 'do you guys build model airplanes,' they all about kill themselves laughing."

Even now Shad and his cronies were clutching their sides and pointing at Yale.

"Look at that, Kresha," Lily said. "Is it worth it to you to sacrifice your view of yourself for some absurd little creep?"

Kresha just smiled at her.

"She doesn't understand that," Suzy said.

"I don't either," Zooey said.

The bell rang then, and Zooey shrugged. "I guess you'll tell us this afternoon."

"Definitely," Lily said. "And until then, no boys, okay?"

As Zooey and Suzy and Kresha walked toward the school building, Reni pointed to Shad and his friends, who had ignored the bell and still had their heads together in what appeared to be heavy conversation.

"They're up to something," she said.

Whatever it was, it didn't reveal itself the rest of the school day, and Lily refused to think about it. Every time she saw one of the Girlz even glancing Shad or Leo or Daniel's way, she cleared her throat loudly, and they shifted their eyes away. All except Kresha. Lily didn't see how she ever got any work done, always working the room with her eyes the way she did. Lily decided they must do that in Croatia a lot too.

When the day finally ended, Lily and the Girlz headed for Reni's, each carrying part of a stack of Lily's library books.

"Ve got to read all these?" Kresha said to her as they hauled them into the newly cleaned clubhouse.

"Just the highlights," Lily said.

When they were all settled on their favorite big pillows, Lily opened a book that was impressively thick.

"Have you read all that already?" Zooey said, eyes bulging.

"Some of it," Lily said modestly. "Enough to know we have a *lot* of work to do. This book says we have to take five steps to good self-image, besides getting rid of the boys, that is."

"Should we write these down?" Suzy said.

"You write it down for us, Sue," Reni said.

Suzy gave a serious nod and took out a binder and a freshly sharpened pencil with an eraser that hadn't even been chewed off yet. Lily had always envied her that quality.

"Okay, step one," Lily said. "Don't let doubts keep you from taking challenges. Got that?"

They all nodded, except for Kresha, who smiled. That was okay. Suzy would translate for her later.

"Step two: Don't assume you'll fail or expect to fail."

She looked at them. Heads nodded.

"Step three: Don't set goals you can't reach. Step four—"

"Wait a minute," Reni said. "I thought you just said we weren't supposed to expect to fail. Now you're saying we shouldn't set too high of goals. Which one's right?"

"What's a goal?" Zooey said.

Lily blew up some air that sent her forehead curls dancing. "Why don't you wait until I'm all done and then you can ask questions."

"What was that?" Reni said suddenly.

"What was what?" Lily said.

Reni shook her head at her and crawled toward the one little window in the clubhouse, which shut out the world with a pair of Suzy's mother's old bath towels they'd tacked up as curtains. She pulled one back to peek out and gasped.

"Toilet paper!"

"You see toilets?" Kresha said.

Lily flung open the clubhouse door—and was hit squarely in the face with something white, wet, and soppy. Behind her, Zooey screamed, Suzy went into hysterical giggles, and Kresha spewed out Croatian. Lily felt sturdy little Reni shove past her and heard her yell, "Shad Shifferdecker! Get out of my yard or so help me—"

Whatever Reni threatened him with was smothered in Shad's grunting laugh, Daniel's snort, and Leo's high-pitched, "We got 'em, dude!"

The clubhouse door slammed, and Reni said, "Those jerks!" between her teeth. Lily could feel somebody, probably Suzy, putting a napkin into her hand. Lily took a swipe at the worst of what was on her face so she could at least see.

"Is that shaving cream?" Reni said.

Zooey scooped up a fingerful from Lily's cheek and popped it into her mouth. "That's whipped cream. Not Cool Whip—this is the stuff from the can."

Kresha and Suzy got to work on Lily's face, and Reni paced.

"There's toilet paper all over," she said, dimples working full time. "And they squirted that stuff on the window and everything. We just cleaned the whole place up. My mama is gonna have a hissy fit!"

"It isn't just that," Lily said. "Look at how violated we've been."

They all stared blankly at her, except Kresha, who, of course, smiled.

"I read that in one of the books," Lily said. "It's like when somebody steals your lunch or something. It isn't about them just taking your sandwich. They do something to *you* when they rip you off or damage your stuff. You feel like they did it *to* you."

Zooey stared at the whipped cream on Lily's chin. "They did."

"I get what you're saying," Reni said. "They didn't just do this to mess up our clubhouse. They did it to mess with *us.*"

Lily pulled away from Suzy, who was trying to get the last of the whipped cream out of her ear, and turned to look at Kresha.

"*Now* do you believe me when I say we have to do without boys *totally?* Do you see what absurd little creeps they can be?"

Kresha shrugged and darted her sharp eyes around at the floor and then finally looked back at Lily.

"Okay, Lee-lee," she said. "No boys."

"Let's make a pledge," Reni said.

They all moved on their knees so they could put their hands together and made a solemn oath that boys were strictly taboo. Then as they pulled the toilet paper off the clubhouse and scrubbed whipped cream from the window, they all agreed it wasn't going to be a hard pledge to keep.

23

But the next day, it turned out to be impossible. It was after first recess, time for social studies. "You won't need your textbooks today," Ms. Gooch said. "We're going to start something different."

Lily's ears practically stood on end. "Something different" usually meant a project, and she loved projects.

"Instead of having you read the chapter on ancient civilizations and answer the questions—which I know you're all getting tired of—we're going to do projects on the various civilizations," Ms. Gooch went on, "and you'll be working in pairs."

Reni shot out her hand across the aisle, and Lily grabbed it. Most of the other girls were doing the same thing. The guys were punching the boys they wanted to work with. Lily could never understand that.

But Ms. Gooch was shaking her head. "You can all relax—I've done the pairing up this time."

Lily immediately felt her heart start to beat faster. This did not have a good sound to it. Suzy was staring in terror at her desktop, and Zooey's eyes looked as if they were about to pop out of her head. Lily started praying.

Please, God, please—don't make me work with Daniel or Leo or Shad. Please—don't let her do that to me—or to any of my friends.

"What if we don't like the person you put us with?" Marcie McCleary was saying.

"Marcie," Ms. Gooch said, "you'll just have to deal with it. It's part of what I want you to learn on this project. You will work together. You will get along. It will be wonderful." Ms. Gooch's left eyebrow went up, and nobody said anything else. The only person left smiling in the room was Kresha. Lily decided she probably had no idea what was going on.

Ms. Gooch took out her roll book. Lily listened and practically dissolved into a relieved puddle on the floor when Ms. Gooch announced that Daniel would be with Chelsea and Leo was assigned to Ashley. Now there was only Shad to go.

"Lily Robbins," Ms. Gooch said. "You'll be working with Yale Phillips."

Lily, of course, nodded at Ms. Gooch. Inside she was thanking God that at least she didn't have to work with Shad.

But *Yale?*

Lily panned the classroom with her eyes and found him in the back. He didn't play mean tricks and make rude comments out loud in class. But poor Yale was so—so not-smart. He could barely spell the easiest words in the spelling bees, and he never got a math problem right on the board.

Even as she was thinking all that, Yale looked up, a slow realization spreading across his small face. He straightened his glasses with one hand and gave her a quick wave with the other.

Oh, brother, Lily thought. *I'm going to end up doing all the work.*

She drummed her fingertips on the desktop as Ms. Gooch finished the assignments. This wasn't going to be good for her self-image, Lily decided. She was going to have to get this changed right away.

Chapter 4

When Lily finally talked to Ms. Gooch at lunchtime, she got two eyebrows . . . *and* a sigh.

"Lily, for heaven's sake," Ms. Gooch said. "I always count on you to be the cooperative one. What's going on with you lately?"

"I'm trying to work on my self-image," Lily said. "And that means I need to reach the goals I've set for myself, and I can't do that if I'm paired up with somebody who can't—who's not—well, you know, who's Yale."

"Lilianna Robbins," Ms. Gooch said. Her eyebrows had all but disappeared up into her black hairline. "Shame on you!"

"I just want to do well," Lily said. "It's about my self-image."

"Where are you getting all this stuff? You sound like a guest on Oprah. Be a kid, would you?"

Lily was confused, but Ms. Gooch didn't give her a chance to ask any questions. "The answer is no, Lily," she said. "I will not give you a new partner. You will figure out a way to work with Yale. Let *that* be your goal."

She stood there with her eyebrows up until Lily nodded and walked away. Lily was nearly to the door when Ms. Gooch said,

"And, Lily, I'm not too worried about your self-image. It's Yale I'm concerned about. You be nice to him, do you hear?"

"Yes," Lily said. She had to bite her lip to keep from saying, *He shouldn't depend on other people for his self-image.* Ms. Gooch obviously wasn't into finding her true self.

At Girlz Only Club that afternoon, all Lily could do was moan.

"Maybe Ms. Gooch would let you trade with me," Zooey said. "I got Lisa, and she doesn't like me. I'm not gonna do that good anyway, so it doesn't matter who I'm with."

Suzy nudged her. "I think that's against one of those rules Lily was teaching us."

"They were steps," Lily said. "That was step two. But I don't *care* about that right now. I want an A on this project, and now it's going to be impossible."

"At least none of us got put with Shad and them," Reni said. She looked at Lily. "Are you still saying we have to ignore them altogether?"

"Why?" Lily said. She saw Reni's eyes dancing, which meant she had an idea of some kind. The other Girlz saw it too, and they were leaning in, even Kresha.

"I got yelled at last night because some of that toilet paper blew out onto the front lawn," Reni said. "My daddy thinks the yard has to be perfect all the time. I hate to get yelled at."

"So what does you getting yelled at have to do with the boys?" Lily said. She was still watching the gleam in Reni's eyes.

"I want to get back at those three," Reni said. "They've been getting away with the stuff they do to us all year. I think it's time for us to get even, because if that happens again, *I* get grounded."

Lily fingered a curl. "I don't know," she said slowly. "That might not be good for our self-image."

"Getting teased all the time and never being able to get even isn't good for *my* self-image, I'll tell you that!" Reni folded her coffee-with-cream-colored arms across her chest. "We can still stay away from them the rest of the time, but I say we do to them what they do to us."

"You mean toilet-paper their houses?" Suzy said. Her forehead was puckered so tight Lily could almost hear it squeaking.

"No," Reni said. "Just find some way to make them look like idiots, which is exactly what they do to us."

"Oh," Zooey said. "Make it so that everybody laughs at *them* for a change."

"Let me see that list of steps, Suzy," Lily said.

Suzy, of course, produced the notebook with the steps neatly printed in pencil—three of them.

"We never got to the fourth one," Suzy said.

Reni grunted. "That's when we got attacked."

Lily frowned at the list. "Well, there's nothing in here that says we *can't* do it."

Reni read over her shoulder. "I think it says we *should*. We shouldn't let our doubts keep us from taking challenges. We shouldn't assume we'll fail. We shouldn't set goals we can't reach—and we *can* do this, Girlz."

"So what would we do?" Suzy said.

"I don't know," Reni said. "But we'll come up with something."

"Lee-lee will think of somesing," Kresha said.

But Lily still wasn't sure. Something about this wasn't quite right, only she couldn't put her finger on it.

She looked up to see them all staring hopefully at her.

"I won't do it unless Lily does," Suzy said.

All right," Lily said. "But we can't do anything too big. We don't want to be creeps like them."

"Right," Suzy said.

"Okay, so we're all in?" Reni said.

Heads nodded.

"So where do we start?" Reni looked at Lily.

"Well," Lily said. It was hard to think. Her heart wasn't in it. "I guess we figure out something that's important to them and go for that. If we pick something that's no big thing to them, they'll just laugh at us."

"That's easy," Reni said. "What do they do, like, morning, noon, and night?"

"Basketbull!" Kresha said.

"Basket*bull?*" Zooey said. "What's that?"

"I heard them talking about a basketball camp they're going to," Suzy said.

"That starts Friday after school—at the middle school," Lily said. "My little brother's going to that too. He's all jazzed about it."

"Perfect," Reni said. "We go to this camp thing and drop water balloons on them—filled with Kool-Aid!"

"In the gym?" Lily said.

Reni dimpled. "Okay, so we sit up in the bleachers and make fun of them."

"You mean, like, yell things?" Suzy said.

"No, just laugh and point. They won't hear what we're saying, but they'll wonder. It'll get them all messed up."

Lily had to admit that would definitely do it. Joe hated to be laughed at when he had any kind of ball in his hand.

"Friday after school in the middle-school gym," Reni said. "Who's in?"

Everybody was. Lily, however, was the last one to raise her hand. There was still something about this that didn't sound quite right.

Maybe I am *letting my doubts keep me from taking challenges,* she thought. *Maybe it's time we just stood up for ourselves.*

That sounded like a self-image thing. In fact, she found it that night in one of the books: "Stand up to people who tease you."

Was that what they were doing, she and the Girlz?

Lily still wasn't sure, and she was getting an unsettled feeling in her stomach.

Maybe I oughta ask Mom, she thought.

She abandoned the book and went downstairs to the family room, where her mother was grading tests. Joe was in there too, supposedly doing his homework.

"You give tests in P.E.?" Joe was saying.

"Softball rules," Mom said. She looked up over the tops of her half-glasses. "Hey, Lil. What lured you out of your library?"

Joe sniffed loudly. "Was it food? Hey, I smell popcorn!"

"I told Art to make some," Mom said.

"Dude—he'll eat it all! Hey, Art, save me some!"

Joe bolted for the kitchen.

"Get a bowl and come right back here and finish these problems," Mom called after him.

"Mom? I have a question for you," Lily said.

"Uh-oh, this sounds heavy," Mom said. "You better go bring *us* some popcorn—I'm going to need brain food for this, I can see that."

"I just want to ask you—"

"Mo-om—Art's hogging it all!" Joe shrieked from the kitchen.

"Go in there and break that up, would you?" Mom said. "And bring the salt."

Lily kept from wailing "Mo-om!" herself. She tried never to lower herself to her brothers' techniques.

There was a losing battle going on in the kitchen when she got there. Art was holding a bowl of popcorn over his head with one hand and examining the cuticles on the other. Joe, about half his older brother's height, was jumping for the bowl, mouth spitting out threats every time he missed, which was every time. Joe had the same mouth as Lily—big, with full lips—though usually it looked more charming

31

on him because he had such a wide face compared with Lily's smaller one. But right now he looked and sounded anything but charming. His brown eyes were narrowed, and his usually every-strand-in-place, brown-sugar hair was flying all over the place.

"Mom says to knock it off," Lily said.

"Hear that, Squirt?" Art said to Joe. "Mom said for you to stop."

"She said for you *both* to stop," Lily said. "And for you to give me some popcorn to take to her."

"You're gonna have to beg me," Art said.

She didn't get a chance to. Art had lost focus just enough for Joe to make a smooth maneuver and take the bowl in one pretty impressive leap. Art lunged for it, but Joe was too quick. He zinged out the door, bowl hugged to his chest, and did an end-zone dance in the dining room.

"Bring that back, ya little—"

"No cussing," Lily said.

Art glared at her as Joe and the popcorn bowl disappeared from view. "Who made you the vocabulary police?" he said.

Lily opened her mouth to whine, but she shut it right away. Words seemed to be tapping on her mental window, trying to get her attention. *Stand up to people who tease you,* the book had said. *Do to them what they do to us,* Reni had said.

"There she goes—she's puckering up," Art said.

"Only because I smell something disgusting," Lily said. "Is that your breath?"

Art's brown eyes blinked. "*My* breath? No!"

"Fine," Lily said. "Let some girl you like get a whiff of that, I don't care."

Art blinked.

"What are you doing, growing the corn?" Mom said from the doorway. "How long does it take to make microwave popcorn?"

"I got mugged!" Art said.

As he and Mom bantered back and forth, Lily smiled to herself and got another bag of popcorn out of the cabinet. That *had* felt pretty good, coming back at Art for once, even if it had slowed him down for only a couple of seconds. It was more than she'd ever been able to do before. Maybe Reni was right after all.

Lily pushed aside the last of the unsettled feeling in her stomach and started planning for Friday.

Chapter 5

Friday couldn't come soon enough for any of the Girlz. For the next two days, they giggled every time they looked at each other, and it already bothered them less when Shad and Leo and Daniel imitated them in voices two octaves too high.

"They won't be laughing Friday," Reni whispered to Lily.

"I know," Lily said, grinning.

The only thing that erased Lily's grin was working with Yale. Just as she'd suspected, he didn't have a clue.

"Okay, we have to do this project on ancient Rome," Lily said. "I was thinking about a Roman newspaper. You know, we could do a sports page about the Coliseum and letters to the editor about Caesar and a fashion page with togas."

"Okay," Yale said. And then he just looked at her, as much as he could from behind the thick, strawberry-blond hair that hung down over the tops of his glasses as if someone had cut it around a bowl on his head. Lily noticed that he had small, very blue eyes that never seemed to blink. It made hers burn just thinking about it.

"Can you look up ancient Roman sports on the computer?" Lily said.

"No," he said, and slunk down into his desk until he looked even smaller than usual. Lily was sure he was littler than Joe, who was only nine.

"What about Julius Caesar?" Lily said.

"Unh-uh."

Well, what can you do? Lily wanted to scream at him.

But instead she said calmly, "Okay then, I'll do the research, and we'll figure out something else for you to do."

Which will probably be nothing, Lily added to herself.

She also decided that it was no wonder Yale had such a lousy self-image. He was anti-step two all over the place.

But Friday finally came and wiped that, and everything else, out of her mind. Right after school, she and the Girlz headed for the middle school, barely able to contain themselves. Zooey didn't, as a matter of fact. She was already laughing so hard that she got the hiccups and insisted she needed a Coke to get rid of them.

Finally they went into the gym and climbed all the way to the top of the bleachers. There were very few other people there, so they figured it would be easy for Shad and Leo and Daniel to notice them.

"I can't wait," Zooey whispered.

"Me neither," Reni said. "This is going to be *good.*"

"Just as long as we aren't going to get in trouble," Suzy said.

"Would you chill?" Reni said. "There's no rule against laughing and pointing in a gym."

"Did you check?" Suzy said.

Reni gave her a dark look, and Kresha patted Suzy on the knee.

"All right," Suzy said, "as long as you're sure."

Several boys trailed into the gym in their shorts and T-shirts then, and Lily squinted to look for Shad and company. These were the littler boys though. In fact, she spotted Joe right away.

"That's my little brother," she said to Kresha. "The one who just grabbed the ball from that other kid."

"Oh," Kresha said, observing Joe carefully. "Cute."

"No—gross," Lily said.

Joe was actually the best-looking one of the Robbins kids, Lily thought, but she didn't have to admit that—especially not to *him*. He hadn't said a kind word about her since he was in kindergarten.

The sixth graders finally came in, and it wasn't hard to pick out Shad. He was wearing baggy shorts that hung on his hips, exposing plaid boxers underneath, and he was, as usual, showing off. As soon as he saw the ball, he shoved Daniel out of the way, grabbed it, and charged the basket doing all kinds of weird circles and gyrations with his arms. When his shot missed—by a mile—he turned around and curled his lip, so that his braces gleamed in the overhead lights.

Lily didn't even have to think about it. She threw her head back and howled. But when she brought it back up and looked, Shad wasn't even looking in her direction, and neither was anybody else.

"He can't hear it if it's just me," Lily said. "Come on, you guys. You have to help me."

"No problem," Reni said. "Do you see how *bad* they are? I think those boys need *glasses.*"

"Yeah," Zooey said. Lily could see little bubbles of spit at the corners of her mouth. "Go to the eye doctor, you guys!" she called down to the court.

Still nobody looked up.

"Everybody at once," Reni said. "Come on, start laughing and pointing. And make it real big."

That they could do, except Suzy. She didn't do anything real big. Kresha was the best at it. Lily decided making fun of people must look the same in any language.

But by the time the coach came in and blew a whistle for the boys to pay attention, nobody had so much as glanced up at the bleachers.

"All right, louder," Reni said.

"I don't think we should do it while the coach is talking to them," Lily said. "They aren't doing anything right now. We'd look stupid."

"I don't want to look stupid!" Zooey said, eyes round.

"Maybe we should move down closer," Suzy said.

Oh," Reni said. She blinked at Lily. "She's right."

So they all moved about halfway down the bleachers and waited for the boys to start moving around and throwing balls again. From there, Lily could even hear the coach talking.

"This isn't about being a star," he was saying. "This is about learning to be a team player. If you're going to play on a team, first you have to have something to offer. That's why we'll spend so much time working on skills. Dribbling, shooting—"

Lily's mind moved on to other subjects. Like the fact that the coach was as tall as a streetlight and like the fact that one of his assistants had to take a ball away from Shad because he wouldn't keep it still while the coach was talking. All the Girlz had to put their hands over their mouths to keep from laughing out loud. This was going to be *so* easy.

Finally the coach wound up his spiel, gave some instructions, and blew his whistle. Boys dribbled and bounced their ways into their age groups—fourth, fifth, and sixth graders—and stood in lines passing the ball back and forth to each other.

"Well, *anybody* could do that," Reni said.

"Yeah!" Zooey said in a loud voice. "What's so hard about that— ya bunch of *babies!*"

This time heads turned. Zooey plastered her hands over her mouth, but Reni gave a huge guffaw and pointed. The rest of the Girlz joined in.

With people finally looking at them, Lily got that unsettled feeling in her stomach again. Until Shad Shifferdecker looked right up at her, and their eyes met. His lip wasn't curled. His eyes weren't cutting slyly from left to right. He wasn't even talking out of the side of his mouth. He looked plain embarrassed. Lily could feel herself breaking into a grin.

She put her hands on either side of her mouth and called out, "I could do that in kindergarten!"

Shad put his head down and drove for the basket. He missed again. The coach blew his whistle.

"Did anybody tell you to take a shot, son?" he said to Shad. "We're doing a passing drill. Now get back in line!"

The Girlz did their best unison laugh yet. Shad glared up at them for a split second and then jogged back to his line with his lip curled.

"We're getting to him!" Reni said. "Keep it up, Girlz!"

They stayed quiet for a few minutes while the coach gave more instructions. The boys all lined up from fourth graders to sixth graders and started another passing drill where they had to dribble and then fling the ball to the person who was running past them. It looked a little complicated to Lily, but she still yelled, "Baby stuff! Grow up, you guys!"

Shad stopped looking at them, but the way he was keeping his neck stiff, Lily could tell he was hearing every word she was saying. Leo and Daniel definitely were, the way they kept turning to look up at the Girlz and missing their passes.

Somebody else was noticing them too. As he ran in place behind the fourth grader stalled in front of him, Joe looked up at the bleachers. He put both hands around his lips and mouthed, "Shut up!"

"You're embarrassing your little brother, Lily," Suzy said.

"Oh, like he's never embarrassed *her* in his life!" Reni said.

"Yeah," Lily said. She looked back down at Joe, just in time to see that while he'd been so busy paying attention to her, the kid in front of him had run on, and Joe was holding up the whole line. Lily put her hand over her mouth and pointed, but Joe didn't look behind him. He just kept sending Lily the lip signal to shut her mouth.

The coach's whistle blew impatiently, and everybody came to a halt.

"All right, people," the coach said, "if you aren't serious about this you need to head for the showers, right now."

He strode across the gym and stood over Joe, looking down at him from his streetlight height. "Why are you here, son?" he said. Below him, cocky little Joe Robbins froze. "Can't hear you, son," the coach said.

"I wanna play basketball," Joe got out in a weak little voice.

"Well, if you want to play ball, you'd better be heads-up and lookin' smart," the coach said. "And that means paying attention to what's going on down here, not what's going on up there."

The coach flung a long arm in the direction of the Girlz and pointed his finger. Lily felt her face going straight to full red, skipping the blotches completely. Suzy stared down at her shoes, and even Kresha stopped smiling. This was the worst.

Or at least it was until the coach whipped his face toward them and said, "You ladies need to leave—now. You're welcome to come back when you learn some manners."

Lily couldn't move. *I'm gonna throw up,* she thought. *No, I'm gonna die. Right here.*

"Come on, Lee-lee," Kresha whispered to her.

Suzy and Zooey were already clattering down the bleachers, and Reni was poking her from behind. Lily stood up and somehow got herself to start moving. The gym was as silent as a class during a spelling test, and she could feel the coach still watching them.

When they got to the gym floor, Kresha said to the coach, "Ve're sorree."

"You just think about it," he said, and then he gave his whistle another insistent toot, and the gym came alive again.

Lily almost ran to the door. When they got outside, Zooey was giggling uncontrollably, and Suzy was swaying back and forth as if she couldn't decide whether to lapse into her own nervous laugh or break into tears. Lily had already chosen the tears.

"Don't cry, Lee-lee," Kresha said. "You make me cry too."

"What are you crying for?" Reni said. "We embarrassed them so bad!"

"But I'm embarrassed too!" Lily said.

"Who knew the coach was gonna hear us?" Reni said.

"Do you think we'll get in trouble?" Suzy said.

Lily looked at Suzy through her tears. "That *was* getting in trouble."

"Joe," Reni said. "He's so gonna tell your parents, isn't he?" Reni smacked her forehead with the heel of her hand. "I'm such a dweeb. I'm sorry, Lily."

"Will they ground you?" Suzy said to Lily.

"I don't know," Lily said. "I never got in bad trouble with them before."

"Wow," Zooey said.

After that, they all walked home in anxious silence.

Lily stayed in her room until it was time to help with supper. Joe didn't get home until they were sitting down at the table. He came straight to the kitchen and flopped himself into his chair without a word. Lily lost her appetite completely.

"Hi," Mom said to him. "Hands."

He flounced to the sink. Lily watched him and prayed, *Please, God, don't let him bring it up at the table. I'll make it up to him, I promise. I'll be so good.* It was an odd thing to remember at that moment, but it suddenly occurred to her that she hadn't been reading the Bible verses Dad had given her along with the books from the library and Mrs. Cavanaugh.

Oh no, she thought. *God's not going to cut me any slack at all!*

She avoided Joe's eyes as he came back to the table and flopped down again.

"It's your turn to say the blessing," Dad said to him.

"Somebody else do it," he said.

"I'll do it for him," Lily said.

She asked God to bless the food and the family—and especially Joe, who'd obviously had a hard day. Then she felt bad about using the blessing to keep Joe from telling on her. Things were so tangled up inside her that she could barely remember the final *Amen*.

"I hate it when she says the blessing," Art said. "The food gets cold."

"There's still steam coming off the broccoli," Mom said. "How about taking some and passing it?"

"So how was your camp, Joey?" Dad said.

Joe shrugged and took the broccoli from Art and passed it on to Mom.

"Help yourself," Mom said dryly.

"I thought you'd be monopolizing the whole conversation," Art said to him.

Silence.

"And I thought you'd be asking what monopolizing means," Mom said. She looked curiously at Joe. "Something wrong, babe?"

"I'm not a babe," Joe said.

"You didn't like the camp?" Dad asked.

"It was all right."

Mom put her hand on his forehead. Joe pulled away.

"I don't think I'm goin' back," Joe said.

"Uh, I beg to differ," Mom said. "Have you forgotten the bucks we forked over?"

"Which you begged for every night for a week," Art put in.

"Let us be the parents, Art," Dad said. He picked up his glasses and looked more closely at Joe. "Did something happen at the camp, son?"

Lily held her breath and prayed, even though she wasn't sure God was speaking to her right now. *Please, God, don't let him tell. Please!*

Joe sat staring at the growing-cold broccoli and didn't move when Art nudged him with the bowl of Rice-a-Roni.

Lily wanted to cry out at him. *I'll do your dishes for a month—I promise!*

And then as if he'd heard her, Joe looked up from his plate and stared at her. His big brown eyes were smoldering.

Here it comes, Lily thought. *I'm sorry, Joe. I'm so sorry.*

Joe shifted his eyes back to his plate and then up at Mom. "I'm not even hungry," he said. "Could I be excused?"

Mom and Dad had one of those conversations with their eyes, and then Dad said, "Sure. You go rest."

"I'll get you something later," Mom said as Joe hurled himself toward the kitchen door.

"Man, it must be nice to be the youngest," Art said. "I never got away with that when I was a kid."

"You never looked that defeated," Dad said. "I wonder what happened?"

"I have an idea," Mom said. "They had Coach Garra doing that camp. I don't necessarily agree with his methods."

"Garra? He's a jerk," Art said.

"I didn't say that," Mom said quickly.

Whatever else she did say, Lily didn't hear it. She just pushed her broccoli back and forth across her plate.

"I'll take Joe up some stuff," she said when they were finished and clearing the table.

Whether it was guilt or relief she felt the most, she didn't know. She just knew she had to be the one to get him alone first.

Chapter 6

"Go away," Joe said when Lily knocked on his door.

She went in anyway. He glared at the tray she put on his bed, but he didn't look at her.

"I didn't put much broccoli on there," she said. "I'll eat it if you want. But I put extra Rice-a-Roni—I mean, since it's your favorite."

Joe sat up on his bed and inspected the plate. "Did you put poison in it?"

"No!" Lily shoved her hair behind her ears. "I'm just trying to be nice to you because you were nice to me. You know, I mean, by not telling Mom and Dad what happened."

Joe finally looked at her. His big, soft eyes were like daggers. "I wasn't doing it to be nice," he said. "I just don't want you telling them I messed up and got yelled at in front of everybody."

The daggers disappeared, and a shine covered Joe's eyes. Lily hadn't seen Joe this close to tears since he was three years old.

"Why'd you have to come anyway?" Joe said. "You made me look like a loser!"

"I didn't mean to!" Lily said.

"Then what'd you come for?"

"We came to—"

Lily caught herself and bit her lip. So far Joe wasn't telling, but what if he did? How much information did she really want him dumping to her parents?

"You came to make me look stupid!" Joe said.

"That's not why I came!" Lily said. "You have to believe me."

"No, I don't. Get out of my room!"

"Not until you promise—"

"I'm not gonna tell on you, okay? Now go away!"

Lily did. She went to her room and flopped down on her own bed and felt as miserable as Joe felt. A self-esteem book slid to the floor, and Lily wriggled to the edge of the mattress to look down at it.

"A lot of good you've done me so far," she said to it. And then she felt a pang of guilt. What about the Bible verses?

She went to her desk and found the list her dad had made for her. The Bible was right there on her bedside table where her parents had taught her to keep it since she'd been out of a crib. But she couldn't pick it up. She felt way too icky to be touching God's Word.

I have to work on my self-image first, she told herself. *And then I'll be good enough to go to God.*

So she opened one of the books from the library and found a section she could understand without having to look up every other word in the dictionary.

"Write down the words from the list below that complete the sentence 'I am,'" she read out loud.

Taking out a sheet of paper, she studied the list. At the moment, none of the words seemed to describe her. She didn't feel especially friendly or fun or loyal right now. She read the directions again.

"Choose the things you really believe you are deep down inside," they said.

Well, I am smart, she decided. *And I am loyal, or I wouldn't be standing up for the Girlz and their self-images.*

She began to write. When she'd finished, she'd put down smart, loyal, sincere, serious, and determined.

She sat up straighter on the bed and read on. "Believe in those qualities in yourself," the book said, "and use them to help you see what you can do."

Lily wasn't sure what all that meant, but she felt better. Maybe tomorrow she'd feel like a good enough person to take a look at a Bible verse or two.

I'll memorize them and everything, she told herself. *Because I am sincere and serious.*

She wasn't certain, but it felt like she might be getting a good self-image.

"I've been thinking about what happened yesterday," Reni said to her before school the next day. "And I think even though we got thrown out of the gym, we still won."

"Nuh-uh!" Lily said. "Shad and those guys watched us get in trouble!"

"Yeah, but they still got embarrassed. At least they know we were willing to take the risk to stand up to them. Isn't that step one?"

"Yeah," Lily said.

"So I think that means we've moved on to step two. We can't assume we failed."

"I'm not sure," Lily said.

"You're letting the doubts take over," Reni said. She stretched her neck way up the way she did when she was really serious. "Don't be doin' that, girl."

"You really think?" Lily said.

"Uh-*huh*, I do."

If Reni thought it, Lily decided maybe she'd better at least consider it. And as the morning got started, it seemed like she might be right. Shad and Daniel and Leo were unusually quiet.

Nothing happened at all until Ms. Gooch got them working on their ancient civilizations projects. Lily was frantically looking up stuff on Roman weapons in the encyclopedia, with Yale sitting next to her, looking unblinking at the pictures, when Daniel brushed past her desk. Lily grabbed the book so he wouldn't knock it off onto the floor, but he only leaned over and whispered, "Watch your back."

"What?" Lily whispered back to him.

But he just went to his seat and picked up a book on the pyramids.

"I wish we'd gotten Egypt," Yale said wistfully.

"Why?" Lily said. "Rome is just as interesting if you'd actually do something."

"What do you want me to do?" Yale said.

She pushed another volume of the encyclopedia toward him. "Can you look up the Coliseum?"

"Nuh-uh," Yale said. "I can't."

Lily frowned and went back to the weapons, but all she could think about was "Watch your back." What did that mean? She glanced around her once, but everybody else was busily working on their projects—except for Shad, who was making a paper airplane.

"They didn't have aircraft in the Byzantine era," Ms. Gooch said as she walked by and took it from him.

"They might have," Shad said. "I saw something about it on the Discovery Channel."

"You're bluffing," Ms. Gooch said. "Get to work."

Shad didn't even look the slightest bit embarrassed.

He's always bluffing, Lily thought. *I bet that "watch your back" thing doesn't mean anything.*

Still, that afternoon at folk dancing time, the minute Ms. Gooch said, "Join hands with your partner," and Lily slid her hand into Leo's, instead of a sweaty palm, she felt a piece of paper. The minute she could do it without Ms. Gooch catching her, Lily looked at it.

Wach yore bak, it said.

"You guys should learn to spell," she said to Leo and shoved the note back into his damp hand.

But when the Girlz met in the clubhouse that day, Lily told them about both incidents.

"They're up to something," Reni said.

"They're going to do something to our backs?" Zooey said.

"'Watch your back' means be careful of what somebody might be doing behind it," Lily said. "You know, without you knowing what's going on."

"Oh," Suzy said gravely. "I hate that."

Lily suddenly put up her hand. "Wait a minute. I found out last night when I was working on my self-image that I'm smart. I think we all are. If we believe that, those boys can't pull anything over on us."

"I don't think 'smart' is *in* my self-imagination thing," Zooey said.

"*Image*," Lily said. "I think we all ought to take the quiz."

"A quiz?" Suzy said. Her nervous giggle slipped out. "Ms. Gooch says I have test anxiety."

"What's that?" Zooey said, eyes round. "I wonder if I have it."

"There's no reason to be scared—there's no grade or anything," Lily said. "It's just how you see yourself."

Kresha grinned and went over to the makeup mirror that Suzy's mother had given them because it didn't work anymore. "I see myself good!" she said.

Lily looked at Suzy.

"I'll help her," Suzy said.

So they all took the quiz, and Lily studied their results.

"Read mine first!" Zooey said. "This is cool!"

"You see yourself as friendly, fun, and loyal," Lily told her.

"Why didn't you circle 'warm'?" Suzy said.

Zooey felt her forehead. "I'm not that warm right now."

49

"No!" Reni said, rolling her eyes. "It means you're nice to people—you don't act all cold to them."

"Oh," Zooey said. "I'm like that?"

"Yes," Suzy said.

"Me, Lee-lee," Kresha said, waving her paper at Lily.

Lily looked from the paper to Kresha. "You circled everything!" she said.

Reni snatched the paper and read off the words and Suzy explained them. Kresha picked friendly, interesting, fun, and sincere.

"You're smart too," Suzy told her. "Look how fast you're learning English. You could hardly speak a word of it when you came here in September."

Kresha tapped her finger with her temple. "Smart?" she said.

"Oh, yes," Zooey said.

Suzy turned out to be loyal, sincere, thoughtful, athletic, and cautious. The Girlz told her to add attractive. She wouldn't.

Reni, they all agreed, was smart, interesting, fun, brave, athletic, and realistic—also sensible.

Lily had them post the lists, including hers, on the clubhouse wall and look at them.

"We're amazing," she said.

"Then we can take anything those boys dish out," Reni said. "Besides, I think they're just trying to scare us. They're being way too obvious about this to really have anything planned."

"You think?" Zooey said.

Lily did, especially after that night when Joe dropped the portable phone in her lap when she was doing her homework and muttered, "For you."

"Lily Robbins?" said a muffled voice when she put the receiver to her ear.

"Yeah?" Lily said. "Who's this?" She didn't know anybody who talked like they had a mouthful of cotton balls.

"Never mind who it is. This is just a warning. Watch your back."

"Shad Shifferdecker, you are so obvious!" Lily said.

But he'd already hung up. Yeah, she decided, Reni was right.

However, the Girlz got together the next morning before school and agreed to watch each other's backs all day, just to be on the safe side.

"We can't get overconfident," Reni said.

"No," Kresha said. She shook her head, as if Reni had said, "We can't eat brussels sprouts ever again."

There wasn't much to watch though. All morning the boys kept their eyes practically superglued to Ms. Gooch.

At first recess, the Girlz were a smug group as they slipped into their sweaters and strolled out to the playground, arm in arm in a line. Ashley and Chelsea passed them and laughed, fingers pointing.

"What's so funny?" Reni said.

Ashley sputtered out a particularly unattractive guffaw, and Chelsea shrieked right along with her. They staggered away, clinging to each other in hysteria, still poking index fingers at them.

"They think we're weird," Suzy said.

"Remember," Lily said, "don't let other people tell you who you are."

They continued off across the playground. Yale hurried past them and then stopped a little ahead. "Ha!" he said, then poked a finger in their general direction and hurried on.

"What was *that* about?" Reni said.

Three more people passed them, cackling and waving fingers, and then another group of four.

"What is going *on*?" Reni said.

"Hey—Lily—you guys!" Marcie McCleary called out from behind them. "How come you all have those signs on your backs?"

Zooey immediately started pawing at the back of her sweater. Lily stopped and swung Reni around. There was, indeed, a sign on her back that read *Laff and point at me.*

"Do I have one?" Lily said.

"Yeah—we all do," Reni said. "They musta put them on when our sweaters were hanging on the backs of our chairs."

"Get it off me!" Zooey cried.

"It's okay," Kresha said. "I vill help."

There was a snort from the direction of the basketball court, and the Girlz all looked. Shad stood there with the ball poised for a shot.

"We told you to watch your backs," he said.

Then he and Daniel and Leo collapsed onto the cement laughing.

"We're not as smart as we thought," Suzy whispered.

"Oh, yes we are," Reni said. "We're smarter than they are, and my self-image is gonna be in big trouble if we don't show them that."

"All right," Lily said. "Everybody start thinking. We're going to get those guys, once and for all."

Chapter 7

Nobody could come up with anything that afternoon at Girlz Only Group, so that night Lily thought about women she knew who were experts on men and whom she might hit up for some advice. The answer was so obvious, she laughed out loud.

Her mother, of course. She had a husband and two sons, and she hardly ever raised her voice. Plus she was a coach and worked with men all the time—even men who were jerks, like Art said about Coach Garra.

Mom and Dad were both in the family room reading the paper when Lily sauntered in, trying to look casual, and draped herself across the couch near Mom's chair. Her mother looked up over the top of the *Burlington County Times*.

"Now what, Lil?" she said. "Do you want to go to acting school?"

"No!" Lily said. "I just want to ask you a question."

Mom put down the paper and picked up her coffee cup. "Okay, shoot," she said. "But don't take too long in the three-second lane."

"Huh?" Lily said.

"Nothing. Ask your question."

"Okay," Lily said. "In what ways do you think women are superior to men?"

"Superior?" Mom said. She twinkled her eyes over at Dad, who was still behind his section of the paper. "I don't actually think women are *superior*. But I think there are some things women are better suited for than men."

"Like what?" Lily said. She wished she'd brought pencil and paper.

"Like having babies."

Well, duh!

"Multitasking—you know, doing more than one thing at a time—and expressing their emotions. Most women—not me, necessarily—can talk about their feelings more easily than men can."

This wasn't helping, and Mom was evidently through because she took a long sip of coffee and put her hand on the paper.

"I've got one, in case anybody's interested," Dad said. He brought the paper down and took off his glasses, sticking them on top of his head. "Women are very good at getting men to do what they want them to do while making the men think it was their idea in the first place."

"We most certainly do not!" Mom said. Lily could see that her lips were getting ready to twitch into a rare smile.

"I'm sorry. I stand corrected," Dad said, and he dove back behind the paper, but not before he gave Lily a wink.

"Don't believe a word he says, Lil," Mom said. "What does he know about women?"

But Lily liked what Dad seemed to know about women. If the Girlz could make Shad and Leo and Daniel do something, only make them think it was their own idea and really get them in the process, what could be better?

It was pretty complex though, she decided, and she didn't want to present it to the girls until she was sure it could work. Otherwise, Zooey alone would ask enough questions to make Lily tear her hair out. Nope, she was going to try it out on somebody first. The most obvious guinea pig was Yale.

What is it I want him to do? she thought the next day while she was doing her math problems in class.

Anything! she answered herself. *If he would just do some of the drawings for our newspaper, except I'd have to get him to trace them because we don't want them to look like a first grader did them.*

Women can make men think it was their own idea, Dad had said.

Lily finished her math problems and went to the stack of thin white paper Ms. Gooch had in the supply area. Then she looked up some big pictures of Roman togas and sharpened a couple of pencils. Even poor Yale couldn't miss this.

When it was time for them to work on their projects, Lily opened the book to the togas and frowned at it, but she didn't say anything. Finally, after the longest pause in life, Yale said, "What's wrong?"

"Well," Lily said, "we can't have a newspaper without pictures, and I can't draw. Oops!"

She pretended to slide on the stack of white paper, and it went to the floor. Yale stared at it, unblinking.

"Could you get that?" Lily said. "I'll probably drop it again."

Yale adjusted his glasses and leaned over and retrieved the paper. He looked at it, his face blank.

"I was going to try to draw on that," she said, "But like I said, I can't draw. Here are some pictures—but I can't make it look like that."

Pretending to do it without thinking, Lily dragged a piece of the paper across the page of the book. "Wow," she said. "This paper is so thin you can see through it. Look at that."

Yale did. And then he said, "I can make it look like that."

Of course you can! Lily wanted to shout. *All you have to do is trace it.* But to Yale she said, "You can? Really?"

He nodded and gathered up the paper and the book and the pencils.

"Where are you going?" she said.

"Over there. I have to spread out," he said. Then, laden with books and paper in his skinny arms, he wove his way around the other students. Shad, of course, stood right in front of him and wouldn't let him pass.

"Hi!" Yale said to him. "Hey, could you teach me how to shoot baskets during recess?"

Lily wanted to groan out loud.

"Sure," Shad said. And then he grunted. "As soon as you grow up."

He grunted again, and Yale practically crawled away and sat down at the art table.

Lily didn't hear a thing from him the rest of the hour, but at least he was drawing. His pencil never stopped the entire time. She was so jazzed that she couldn't wait to tell the Girlz.

"I've got it!" she told them at lunchtime. "We have to decide what we want those boys to do that will make them look really stupid, and then we have to make them come up with the idea themselves from suggestions we give them. Only they can't sound like suggestions."

"What?" Zooey said.

Lily told them about Yale, and then even Zooey got it. By the end of their Girlz Only meeting, they had a plan.

"We're getting positive self-images, Girlz," Lily told them.

"Self-imach!" Kresha said. "I like dat!"

They decided to put the plan into play at afternoon recess the next day, and by then they were ready. They'd been over every step at least a dozen times.

Just before recess, Reni asked if she could go to the restroom. Lily saw her pick up her backpack on the way out and noted the smile on her face when she came back. So far, so good.

As soon as the bell rang, the boys bolted from the building as usual, and the Girlz gathered around Reni and her backpack. Suzy, Kresha, and Reni put on the gloves she gave them.

"Do this fast," she said, "or it'll start to dry and you won't be able to pull loose."

The three of them made a run for it, and Zooey and Lily followed, looking around to make sure nobody suspected anything. Zooey could hardly contain herself, but Lily nudged her every time she started to laugh too loud, and she plastered her hands over her mouth.

There was reason to laugh. The plan was going perfectly. Reni, Suzy, and Kresha, each with gloves on, were quickly working their way from one end of the parallel playground bars to the other. Suzy was really moving along, legs swinging high above the ground. It was perfect, Lily thought, that she was in gymnastics.

Reni, who could play just about any sport, was moving effortlessly right behind her, although Lily knew she was being careful not to put her hands right where Suzy had put hers. It wasn't hard because she could probably see the heavy-duty adhesive Suzy had deposited there with her gloves.

And filling in the spaces right behind them was wiry Kresha, whose thin arms hid sinewy muscles that were up for the task.

"They're doing it!" Zooey squeaked to Lily.

"Yeah, but where are the boys?" Lily said.

She looked nervously around the playground. If the boys didn't jump up there soon and try to outdo them, the glue was going to dry and the whole plan would be ruined.

But they hadn't figured the boys wrong. Shad was at that moment tearing over from the basketball court with his friends right behind him. A crowd had gathered under the parallel bars, and they obviously weren't going to miss out on some attention.

Lily looked back at Suzy. She had seen them too, and she was doing exactly what they'd told her to. Just before she got to the end of the bars, she executed a flip that drove the crowd wild.

"Wow!" Marcie McCleary cried over everyone else. "I didn't know she could do that!"

Ashley sniffed. "I didn't even know she was in our class."

Suzy did a fancy dismount. Lily was there to take her gloves. They had agreed to dispose of the evidence as soon as possible.

Not to be outdone, Reni did a flip too and jumped down grinning. The crowd clapped and then howled as Kresha pretended to fall and ended up hanging upside down. She let the gloves drop, and Lily picked them up. She handed them to Zooey, who hurried away toward the trash can. If anybody noticed, they didn't say anything. They were all staring at the trio who had just enthralled them.

"How do you *do* that?" Marcie said.

"Oh, it's easy," Reni said. "For girls, that is. Boys can't do it."

"What?" Shad said.

Lily bit her lip to keep from grinning.

"Boys can't do it," Reni said. "You're built different, and you can't do it."

"Bull-loney!" Shad said. He punched Leo, and Leo joined in with a, "Who says?" Daniel piped up with, "That's pretty stupid!" before he could be punched too.

"Fine, don't believe me," Reni said.

"I don't!" Shad said.

"Then show them, Shad," Ashley said. "I hate it when they talk like they know everything."

Yeah, show us, Shad, Lily thought. *And hurry up before the glue dries!*

"Dude, this is lame," Shad said.

He swaggered his way to the end of the bars and gave the crowd an I-can't-believe-I'm-even-wasting-my-time look. Lily held her breath.

Shad jumped without effort and grabbed onto the bars. He moved one hand, then the other, and Lily's heart started to sink. But then abruptly, he stopped. Lily could see the muscles in his arms working.

"So what's that?" Marcie said. "Are you going to do a flip?"

"Yes," Shad said tightly.

Then his arms worked some more, but they didn't move. Reni stood behind Lily and pulled at her sweater. Lily nodded and grabbed for Kresha's arm. Suzy and Zooey joined them in a we-have-to-keep-ourselves-from-laughing knot.

"Whatsa matter, dude?" Leo said.

"I'm stuck!" Shad said. "Come up here and get me!"

Leo went obediently to the other end of the bars, where Shad hadn't been yet, and jumped up. In seconds, he was dangling help-lessly too.

"There's something on here!" Leo cried. "Dan—dude—get us off!"

By now the whole crowd was screaming, and Daniel leaped right up onto the bars between them and was immediately fastened by the hands. He kicked to try to free himself and got Shad right in the buns. That drove the crowd wild.

"Look at their pants!" Suzy whispered to Lily.

Three pairs of baggy pants were slowly crawling down over the boys' almost-not-there hips, the hips that were stretched even thinner by the position they were in.

"Leo!" Marcie shouted. "We can see your underwear! Yours too, Daniel!"

"Nice boxers, Shad!" Ashley and Chelsea called out in unison.

"Pull 'em up!" Shad called back. But nobody did because everyone was laughing too hard, the Girlz included. This was a development they *hadn't* planned, and it was too perfect.

Just then the bell rang, and almost as if on cue, Leo's and Daniel's pants slid off and ended up in piles on the ground. Everyone scattered, leaving the three of them dangling from the bars, two of them pantless.

"Let's go!" Suzy whispered, and she took off toward the building like a shot with the rest of the Girlz behind her.

But Lily couldn't stand it. She couldn't leave it alone. This was too, too good, and she had a lot of scores to settle with Shad Shifferdecker. Still laughing, she ran up to Shad and gave his pants the final yank, leaving him boxer-exposed to the rest of the playground.

"Got you, Shad Shifferdecker!" she cried, and then she turned around to run. She plowed right into a figure with one big eyebrow.

"Got *you*, Lily Robbins," said Ms. Gooch.

Chapter 8

Lily had never seen the inside of the principal's office. She could barely see it now for the tears she was fighting back. All she really took in was Mr. Ronald, who sat on the edge of his desk and looked down on her in the chair.

"I'm surprised to see you in here," he said. "Surprised and disappointed."

Lily couldn't say anything. All the held-back tears were clogged up in her throat.

"Ms. Gooch seems to think you know something about what happened out there on the parallel bars," he said. "Is that true?"

Lily tried to clear her throat, but that only brought more tears. She swiped at her cheek and managed to say, "I did pull Shad's pants the rest of the way down. But they were already falling."

"I'm not talking about that," Mr. Ronald said. His voice grew tighter and so did his mouth. "I'm talking about the three boys who have been glued to the bars. I've got a janitor and a school nurse out there trying to get them down without tearing the skin off their hands, and I'd like to know how they got in that predicament."

"Tearing the skin off?" Lily said. "I didn't know it would do that!"

Mr. Ronald nodded and folded his hands. "So why don't you tell me what you *did* know," he said. "I always go easier on students who tell me the truth."

Lily thought it would be a whole lot easier if she waited until the other Girlz came in here and confessed with her. Maybe if she stalled, he'd wait until they got here.

"What is there to think about?" Mr. Ronald said. "Just be honest. Let's go."

Okay, so much for stalling. She'd tell her part of the story, and then they could tell theirs when they came in, and it would all fit together.

"I wanted to get back at Shad Shifferdecker and those guys for teasing me all the time," Lily said. "You wouldn't believe some of the things they've done to me and my friends."

"Let's stick to what *you* did," Mr. Ronald said.

Lily nodded. "Okay—so I put some industrial glue on gloves and—*stick to my story—let the other girls tell theirs—they'll be here any minute*—and it got on the bars and then those guys got up there and got stuck. But I didn't know it could be dangerous and really hurt them! I just wanted them to look stupid."

There was a tap on the door, and Lily begged it with her eyes to open and bring in the Girlz. But it was the nurse. Mr. Ronald went over to her, and they whispered for a minute.

"You're lucky, Lily," Mr. Ronald said. "There's been no injury to the boys. Otherwise, your parents could have been looking at a lawsuit."

"My parents!" Lily said.

"And *you* would have been looking at a suspension."

The tears came now, and Lily didn't even try to stop them. Mr. Ronald handed her a box of Kleenex from his desk.

"Don't get all upset," he said calmly. "Ms. Gooch tells me that you are usually a perfect student and citizen, so I'm not going to suspend you. However, from what I see, you are far from perfect."

"I know!" Lily blubbered. She had no self-image left by this time.

"Since Ms. Gooch knows you better than I do, and since she assures me nothing like this is ever going to happen again with you—"

"No, it won't!"

"I'm going to ask her to keep you after school every day next week and deal with you as she sees fit. I'm urging her to help you work on whatever it was that made you pull a stunt like that."

"I will—I'll change!" Lily said. She wiped away the goo that was pouring out of her nose and stood up to leave, but Mr. Ronald wasn't finished with her.

"I know you didn't pull off this caper by yourself," he said. "Are you going to tell me who helped you?"

Lily couldn't even force herself to answer. Mr. Ronald nodded.

"That's what I thought," he said. "But friends aren't friends if they let you take the rap for something they were involved in too. If you change your mind, this door is always open."

Lily went straight to the bathroom and sobbed. Ms. Gooch found her there.

"Lily, I don't know what's going on with you," she said, "but I think we ought to find out and get it fixed. Now, I've called your mother—"

"You called my mom?" Lily said. She looked miserably down at the toilet. If only she could flush herself down it.

"I did, and she sounded as disappointed as I am. We both agree that this self-image kick you're on has gone way too far." Ms. Gooch let her eyebrows come down. "A positive self-image is supposed to make you behave better, not worse. Frankly, I didn't see anything wrong with the one you had before." She gave Lily's shoulder a pat. "One good thing has come out of this, anyway. I've decided to make a bigger deal out of the IALAC thing than I'd planned to. Anyway—" Another pat. "Wash your face and come join us in the multipurpose room."

"Do I have to dance today?" Lily said.

"Oh, yes, my dear."

"Ms. Gooch?"

Ms. Gooch stopped at the bathroom door, and Lily took a huge breath. "Has anybody else said anything to you about what happened on the playground?"

"I've heard nothing else since, trust me."

"But I mean—"

Lily stopped. It was no use. If the Girlz had confessed, Ms. Gooch would have said something by now. It looked like she was going to be staying after school all by herself.

But that wasn't even the worst part, Lily thought as she splashed cold water on her permanently blotchy face. The worst part was the hurt that they were letting her take all the blame.

That was all she could think about as she walked reluctantly across the multipurpose room and stood beside Leo with his hands that now smelled like Neosporin instead of sweat. She didn't even care that most of the class was staring at her and snickering to each other. She only cared that none of her friends—not Kresha, Zooey, Suzy, or even Reni—would look at her at all.

With all that going on in her head, it was impossible to concentrate on the tarantella. When Ms. Gooch called out for the girls to form one line and the boys another so they could learn to weave in and out, Lily moved in a daze to stand behind, of all people, Marcie McCleary.

"I bet you got in *so* much trouble," she whispered to Lily behind her hand. "Did you get a suspension?"

Lily shook her head and looked the other way.

"Now begin to weave!" Ms. Gooch shouted over the music.

At least that put somebody else between Lily and Marcie. But that somebody was Shad. Lily jerked to attention, but not soon enough. Shad put his mouth close to her ear and said, "You've had it now, Snobbins."

He gave her a shove on the arm that sent her reeling right into Ashley Adamson.

"Watch it! Knock it off!" Ashley yelled at her.

If Lily could have, she would have, but Shad's push was so hard, Lily couldn't get her balance, and she finally went to the ground—right at Reni's feet.

Reni couldn't help it this time; she had to look at Lily. She looked away so fast that the little pigtails on her head quivered. But it wasn't before Lily saw her eyes. She didn't look brave or sincere or strong or any of those things in her self-image profile. She looked scared and ashamed. There was no way she was going to tell on herself, and Lily knew it.

The music had been snapped to a stop by this time, and Ms. Gooch was nose to nose with Shad.

"Did you push her down?" Ms. Gooch said.

"He did—I saw it," Marcie said.

"I want to hear it from Shad," Ms. Gooch said.

"After what she did to me, what's a little shove?" Shad said.

"Yeah," Leo said.

From somewhere in the room, Daniel snorted.

"How many different voices does Shad have?" Ms. Gooch said. She raised both eyebrows at the entire class, and they quieted like a tomb.

"Quite frankly I am sick of this feud between the two of you." She swept her eyes over Lily and back to Shad. "I want it stopped. Shad, you will stay after school every day next week *with* Lily. By Friday I want your differences worked out, or there will be more consequences to come—for both of you."

Once more she looked at Lily, who couldn't move for fear she'd burst into sobs right there in front of everyone. She swallowed hard, got to her feet, and took her place in the line behind Marcie. Shad muttered under his breath and gave Ms. Gooch dark looks as she marched back to the tape deck. But they were nothing compared with the ones he shot at Lily when he knew the coast was clear.

Still, *that* was nothing compared with the looks she got that night and all weekend at home.

Mom was madder than Lily had ever seen her. She couldn't even talk about it for the first hour Lily was home Friday afternoon. She just sent Lily to her room, and Lily could hear her in the kitchen below, slamming cabinet doors as she put away the groceries.

Art poked his head into Lily's doorway—something he never did unless he needed to borrow something—and said, "Why is Mom down there throwing cans? Did some kid give her grief today?"

"Yes," Lily said, but she sure wasn't going to tell him who.

"What's the matter with you?" he said.

"Nothing," Lily said.

"You lie like a rug," Art said. "Did one of your little girlfriends steal your boyfriend or something?"

"No! I hate boys! All of them!"

Lily picked up a pillow and hurled it at him, but he managed to get the door shut to block it.

"Your hormones must be kicking in," he said from the hallway. "I gotta think about getting my own place."

By the time Dad got home, Mom was talking again. And, man, was she talking. As Lily stood in front of them in the family room, she decided she liked the silent treatment better.

"What on earth were you thinking, Lilianna?" Mom said. "Didn't you realize you could have seriously hurt one of those boys?"

"No!" Lily said. "I wouldn't have done it if I'd known that!"

"Why *did* you do it? That's what I want to know." Dad's face, unlike Mom's, looked sad and disappointed. That was almost worse than Mom's blazing eyes and her more-than-a-little-bit-raised voice.

"I wanted to get back at them for teasing me all the time," Lily said. "I wanted them to feel stupid, the way they always make me feel."

"Oh, for heaven's sake, they're just immature boys. You ought to know what boys are like by now—you live with two of them every day." Mom shook her head until her ponytail tossed. "It makes absolutely no sense to me. You're so much smarter than that."

Dad put his hand on Mom's arm, and she clamped her mouth shut as if that were the last thing she wanted to do.

"I want to understand exactly what happened out there," Dad said. "Because, like your mother, I can't comprehend what you were thinking. Now start from the beginning. Come on and sit down. Tell us the story."

Lily looked at him in horror.

"Sit, girl," Mom said. "It isn't a difficult concept."

I can't! Lily wanted to shout at her. *I can't sit down and tell you the story because I can't tell on my friends! I won't! I don't care if they are letting me take all the blame. I won't be a tattletale.* After all, this was *her* self-image, not theirs.

"Let's hear it," Mom said.

"Can't I just take my punishment?" she managed to say. "I did wrong. I was horrible . . . and I don't want to talk about it."

"We can't give you a punishment if we don't know exactly what the crime was," Dad said.

Lily was surprised at how firm his voice sounded. She looked at him. He was drilling his blue eyes right into her, and it made her want to cry again. She had never seen him this serious with her before. But then, she'd never been in this much trouble with him before.

"There was this idea," Lily said finally, slowly, "that if there was industrial adhesive on gloves and that stuff got on the bars and then the boys got on it, they would stick, just long enough to look stupid. I really never thought—"

"Industrial adhesive?" Mom said. "Where on earth did you get something like that?"

Lily froze.

"Tell me we're not talking stealing it from the janitor!" Mom said.

"No!" Lily said. "I got it from Zooey."

That was the truth. Zooey had gotten it from her garage. Her dad did some kind of work where he put down floors or something.

"Zooey didn't ask what it was for?" Dad said.

Lily shook her head. That was true too. Zooey had already known what it was for.

"And the gloves?" Dad said.

"Reni," Lily said. Her father's old gardening gloves.

"Now, I can't *believe* Reni didn't ask questions!" Mom said.

"Lilliputian, is there something you aren't telling us?" Dad said.

Lily let herself breathe. Dad was calling her "Lilliputian" again.

"We just want you to be honest with us," Mom said. "All this stuff about self-image means absolutely nothing if you can't tell the truth about yourself and what you've done."

"Let me ask you something," Dad said.

Oh, please don't! Lily thought.

He chewed on the earpiece of his glasses and then said, "Have you been reading the Bible verses I gave you?"

Lily shook her head miserably.

"Ah, then there's our problem," he said. "And I think this is our solution. You are grounded for the weekend and all of next week. No TV. No phone."

That means no Girlz! Lily bit her lip.

"I want you to spend all the time you're at home in your room—unless you want to talk to your mother or me about all this. And while you're in there, I want you to spend some time on those verses. Now—" he put his glasses on and looked at her closely. "This part is *not* a punishment. This is the learning that we want to take place as a result of your time alone. You do understand that?"

"Yes," Lily said.

"And no more self-image books," Mom said. "They all go back to the library and to Mrs. Cavanaugh."

"There is nothing wrong with self-help books," Dad put in, "if you know how to use them. I don't think you do yet, and I should have listened to your mother on that in the first place. We need to start with the basic self-help Book so you can judge everything else from that."

Lily nodded again, but she really didn't care. The only image she had of herself right now was of a stupid, bad person who didn't even have friends who would stand up for her. She was turning into a kid just like Shad Shifferdecker.

"Lil, don't cry," Mom said.

She handed Lily a Kleenex. Lily hadn't even realized she *was* crying. She blew her nose and felt Dad patting her on the leg.

"We love you," he said. "Otherwise we wouldn't be trying so hard to make sure this all turns out right—that you learn from it."

"Can I go to my room now?" Lily said.

They let her go, and Lily fled. She ran into Joe on the stairs.

"Just don't say anything, all right," she said. "I can't handle it right now."

"Who said I was even speaking to you?" he said.

Lily continued up the steps two at a time and locked herself in her room, where she sobbed into her pillow.

"I hate boys!" she cried. "I never want to see one again!"

But what was worse—what kept the tears coming and coming—was that right at that moment, she hated herself even more.

Chapter 9

By the end of the weekend, Lily was pretty sick of herself. She couldn't talk to the Girlz on the phone, and she wasn't so sure she wanted to speak to them anyway. They didn't even try to call her. She had asked her mom about that.

"I think they sense you're under house arrest," Mom said.

The pile of self-image books was gone too, and Lily had read all her other books a dozen times and gotten her homework done by ten o'clock Saturday morning. There was nothing else *to* do except read the Bible verses—not that she wouldn't have anyway. She was trying to do everything exactly right so her parents would stop being so disappointed in her.

Lily herself was disappointed that the Bible wasn't as easy to understand as the self-image books. There were no quizzes to take or checklists to fill out and no case histories of girls who'd found their self-images.

Dad had given her verses like Matthew 5:3–10 or Matthew 5:14–16, where Jesus told people to be content with what God wanted them to be.

Yeah, but I'm not a good person! Lily thought. *I can't be content with that.*

And then there was another place in Matthew where Jesus told the people not to pay any attention to other people's opinions but to listen to God.

But he's not telling me anything!

Dad had also included one more from Matthew in which Jesus said God sees the real us. He loves us for who we are and what we will become.

I sure hope so, Lily thought. But she wasn't sure she believed it. After all, she had practically stopped praying altogether.

One group of verses did make some sense to Lily. It said to cast out evil, and you've got it made. Say no to evil and chase it off, or better yet, tie it up. You have to be filled with God—leave no room for evil.

Lily wasn't sure what that had to do with self-image, but at least it sounded like something she could do, and she was willing to give it a try. She practiced on Art when he came by to tell her Sunday supper was ready.

"Don't throw anything at me," he said. "I'm just the messenger."

She took a deep breath. "I'm sorry I did that the other day."

"Solitary confinement makes you do weird stuff." He leaned on the doorjamb. "So what have you been doing in here all weekend, writing a novel?"

Lily shrugged. She definitely wasn't going to tell him she'd been reading the Bible and then have him laugh at her. She'd have to throw something at him.

"I used to get grounded a lot when I was in middle school," Art said. "I was in my rebellious period. I grew out of it." Art gave half a grin. "Every time I got sent to my room for, like, fifty years, I'd get so bored that I'd clean it up. I think that's why Mom used that punishment so often. It was the only time you could see the floor."

Lily looked around at her neat bookshelves and the tidy top of her dresser. "Mine's always clean," she said.

"Yeah, well, you're little miss always-do-everything-right anyway."

"No, I'm not!" Lily said. "I hardly do anything right anymore!"

"You really oughta consider switching to decaf, Lil," he said. "You do more stuff right than anybody I know. You make me sick, you're so perfect."

Any other time, Lily would have thought about it and decided that was a compliment. But right now, nothing sounded good, and besides, she had to concentrate on tomorrow at school and how she was going to avoid evil—no, tie it up—so she could be pure and good. And make room for God. She had to do it all.

But as she lay in bed that night, the shadows fell across her mind again. What if the Girlz still wouldn't even talk to her tomorrow? What if they were so scared of her telling on them, they just stopped being her friends? Who would be her friends then?

The tears welled up again because there wasn't anybody else she wanted as friends. Kresha, Zooey, Suzy—and Reni—were her favorite people. They'd already promised to be in each other's weddings—if there were actually any decent boys out there, which they all doubted.

Lily tossed in bed. She really was going to have to study that Bible verse and try to do what it said. If she was going to have to spend every minute with herself, she'd better be somebody she at least liked.

Wouldn't it be horrible to be somebody like Shad—somebody there was no hope of liking?

And then she sat up straight and stared at the dark wall.

But I've turned into Shad! she thought. *I'm just like him—full of pranks and hate and . . . and . . . evil!*

She flopped back down into the pillows and squeezed her eyes shut. *Make room for God,* the verse had said.

She shoved thoughts of Shad out of her mind and started to pray.

When Lily got to school on Monday, she went straight to the classroom so she wouldn't have to see the Girlz all standing in a group on the playground talking without her. Big mistake. Shad was there—with his mother.

The woman's face had deep scowl marks in it, and she was talking to Ms. Gooch in the kind of voice that Lily's mom used only when she was yelling at a referee.

"I just want to make sure everything is being done fairly," she was saying.

Shad was slouched next to her, playing with the stapler on Ms. Gooch's desk. Lily slipped into her desk and cleaned out her binder.

"I mean, I know you're fair, don't get me wrong," Mrs. Shifferdecker went on, "but when the kid comes home and tells me he got glued to the monkey bars in one breath and that he has to stay after school every day in the next breath, I wonder, you know what I'm saying? Now I know he can be a pain. I'm on him at home all the time. Aren't I?"

Lily glanced up to see her plucking at Shad's sleeve. He pulled away and replaced the stapler with the tape dispenser as his plaything. Lily went back to her vocabulary list and was glad Mrs. Shifferdecker wasn't *her* mother.

"But I don't want everything blamed on him. I mean, I want to make sure you aren't just assuming that Shad provoked this person—whoever it was, he won't tell me—to try to glue him to the bars. If he did, he'll get punished, but I have to make sure."

Lily was stunned. Shad hadn't told his mother it was Lily who'd done it to him?

"So why's he being kept after?" Mrs. Shifferdecker said.

"Didn't you tell your mother, Shad?" Ms. Gooch said.

Shad closely examined the tape dispenser. His mother snatched it out of his hand and slammed it down on the desk.

"Answer her!" she said.

"I pushed somebody—but it was by accident!"

"Who did you push?"

"It don't matter!"

"*Doesn't* matter—"

"Whatever."

"I hate that 'whatever' business. Now you tell me—"

"Mrs. Shifferdecker," Ms. Gooch said. "The bell is about to ring and other children are going to be coming in." She evidently hadn't noticed Lily who now slid down in the desk chair. "I'm satisfied that justice is being done, if you are."

"Oh, like I said, I'm sure you're being fair—"

Mrs. Shifferdecker went off on another paragraph, and other kids did start to file in. Shad went from slouching to showing off, putting the tape dispenser on top of his head, then catching it and trying to juggle it with the three-hole punch. Ms. Gooch calmly took them away from him and guided Mrs. Shifferdecker by the arm toward the door.

"Busted!" Leo called out to Shad from the back of the room.

"Yeah, well, I'm not the only one—finally," Shad said. And his eyes glittered on Lily.

Daniel snorted, and Marcie leaned over Lily's desk and said, "I feel so sorry for you."

"Thanks," Lily said dully.

She would have liked it a lot better if those words had come from one of the Girlz. But they all waited until the bell was about to ring before they rushed in and scooted into their seats. Not one of them even looked at her.

It was your idea! Lily wanted to scream at Reni. But she didn't. She had to cast out evil—tie it up. She nibbled her lower lip.

By the time Ms. Gooch set them to work on their ancient civilizations projects, Lily was almost in tears again. Loneliness, she decided, hurt worse than an earache or something. But there was a surprise that, for the moment, eased the pain a little.

As Lily pulled a desk over next to Yale's, she noticed that he had something out on his.

"Are those the toga pictures you traced?" she said hopefully.

"Unh-uh," he said.

So much for getting men to do what you wanted them to do by making them think it was their idea.

"I didn't trace them," he said as she slid into the desk. "I drew my own. Is that okay?"

Lily stared at the drawings Yale held out to her. They were lively pictures of Romans dancing across the page in flowing togas and leafy headpieces. He had everything perfect, right down to the funky hairstyles on the men.

"You did these?" Lily said.

"Uh-huh."

"You didn't trace them—you drew them by yourself?"

"Uh-huh." Yale pushed his glasses up on his nose. "I still have to color them in, but that's easy."

"Why didn't you tell me you could draw like this?" Lily said.

Yale shrugged. "You didn't ask me."

"But I asked you all that other stuff and you said no, so I just thought—"

Lily stopped herself before she spit out, *so I just figured you couldn't do* any*thing*. She didn't have to. The way Yale ducked his head, she knew he'd heard it in her voice anyway.

She was liking herself less and less by the minute.

Morning recess and lunch were horrible without the Girlz. Lily asked Ms. Gooch if she could do her after-school detention during afternoon recess, but she said no, so once again Lily stood alone against the wall and tried not to watch the Girlz sitting under the tree. By the time the class went into the multipurpose room for folk dancing, the thought of dancing with Leo was just too much for her.

"Ms. Gooch," Lily said when everyone was getting into formation, "couldn't I *please* have a different partner?"

"What is the *matter* with you, child?" Ms. Gooch said. Her eyebrows were fully operational. "You're not getting it, are you? You are so much better than this—all this stuff that you've been doing lately. Now get along with Leo, or don't dance."

"I can't," Lily said.

"Then don't. All right, people—"

The dancing started. Ms. Gooch put a girl whose partner was absent with Leo, and the whole thing went on without Lily. She sat on the floor against the wall and tried not to watch. Every time she did, she caught one of the Girlz sneaking a glance at her. And every time, their eyes looked guilty.

But they didn't tell. It was Lily alone who stayed in her desk that afternoon when the bell rang and everyone left. Lily alone—with Shad.

Ms. Gooch made them sit side by side in the front row, and she leaned against her desk with her arms folded and both eyebrows up.

"All right, you two," she said. "The goal for this week is for you to learn to respect each other so that it will not be so difficult for you to be civil to one another."

"Aw, man!" Shad said. "Can't I just write somethin' a hundred times?"

I'll do a book report, Lily thought. *I'll do two!* But she didn't say it. She didn't want to be like Shad anymore.

"What do you want us to do?" she asked.

"I want you to take down the bulletin board. Together."

"But, I mean, what do you want us to do to learn to respect each other?"

"That's it," Ms. Gooch said. "Go for it."

"Then after we're done, can we go?" Shad said.

"One step at a time," Ms. Gooch said. She handed Lily a staple remover. "Have at it," she said.

Lily marched right over to the board and began ripping out staples with a vengeance. She didn't care if she had to rip out her own nose hairs with red-hot tweezers. She had to get Ms. Gooch to think she was a good person again.

No, she had to *be* a good person. *I'm trying to make room for you, God,* she thought. She glanced at Shad, who was scowling as he tried to pry the little letters off with his dirty fingernails. *But could you have made it any harder?*

Chapter 10

When Lily had almost finished picking off all the small letters on her side and was ready to go after the bigger stuff underneath, Shad was still pulling at his first word.

He curled his lip back over his braces, and his snappy little eyes seemed to draw closer together. "Did I ever tell you it creeps me out when you stare at me all weird like that?"

"Yes," Lily said. "About a million times." She glanced uneasily over her shoulder. Ms. Gooch had gone into her office. "We have to get this done," Lily said. "Here, use this—it's easier."

She held out the staple remover, but Shad shook his head. "I got a better idea. You take off all the small stuff, and I'll rip off the big stuff. My fingers are too big or somethin'."

"Oh," Lily said. It did sound like a good idea, and Shad had the first three big pieces torn off in about fifteen seconds. Lily went behind him pulling out staples. Maybe if they finished in record time, she thought, Ms. Gooch would say they didn't have to come back anymore the rest of the week because they had cooperated with each other.

"So, what was that stuff anyway?" Shad said.

"What stuff?" Lily said.

"That goop that stuck me to them bars."

"Industrial adhesive," she said.

"What's that?"

"Glue you use to put down floors in kitchens and stuff."

"Where'd you get it?"

Lily bit her lip and focused on an especially stubborn staple.

"That's what I thought," Shad said. "How come you didn't tell on them?"

"Who?"

"Them girls that's in your club or whatever it is."

Lily stopped and stared at him. "How did you know we had a club?"

"I saw it on the sign—except you spelled 'girls' wrong. It don't got a Z on the end."

"You saw it that day you guys tee-peed our clubhouse?" Lily said. "And threw whipped cream in my face?"

"So gluing us to the bars was like a payback?" Shad said.

Lily shrugged.

"Then your friends *were* in it with ya."

"What friends?"

"Yeah," Shad said. He curled his lip again. "What friends? If they was really yer friends, they'd of turned themselves in by now. Leo and Daniel, they'd never let me go down by myself."

Lily didn't answer him. She knew he was right.

When they were finished, Ms. Gooch let them go home, but there was no talking her out of the rest of the week.

"I didn't hear any screaming in here," she said, "so you're making progress, but you still have a long way to go. I'll see you tomorrow."

On her way home, Lily didn't notice the puddles or the warm air or any of the daffodils that were peeking up out of people's gardens.

She mostly walked with her head down, looking at the cracks in the sidewalk with unseeing eyes. She stopped to notice something only once—and that was when she passed Reni's house.

The window in the clubhouse was open, and voices drifted out like the chattering of squirrels. Lily heard Suzy's nervous giggle and Zooey's voice going up into a whine about something, and she could even hear Kresha saying, "It's okay. It's okay."

But the thing that threatened to tear Lily's heart right out was Reni's voice, strong and firm above the others, saying, "No, it is *not* okay!"

She's president now, Lily thought. *They've just gone on without me like I was never even there.*

She went straight to her room when she got home so she could cry without anybody seeing her.

They must have never liked me in the first place! She told herself. *Or they couldn't forget about me so fast.*

"God?" she said out loud. "Will you please let me be somebody I can like?"

Suddenly there was a warm hand on her back and a voice was saying to her, "How about somebody *God* can like? Maybe the person *he* wants you to be."

Lily rolled over and looked at her mother through puffy eyes. "It's supposed to be my *self*-image though. I'm supposed to like who I am."

"You can't like it if God doesn't like it, I know that for a fact," Mom said. "Let's call it—instead of self-image—God-image. You figure out who it is God wants you to be and be it, and you've got it made."

"But how do I do that?"

"Be yourself."

"But I don't know who that is! You do, and Dad does, and Art and even Joe—you all know exactly who you are. I don't!"

"I think you're working at it too hard, Lil," Mom said. "Just let it be."

But that was like asking her to let Yale do the Roman newspaper project while she sat back. She couldn't do either one.

The next day in school when they were working on it, Lily said, "Aw, man, we don't have any pictures of Roman weapons to put with this war story. Maybe I could get some off the Internet."

"I could draw them," Yale said.

"I know," Lily said, "but I don't have a picture for you to copy. I know they're on the Internet though because I saw them that one day."

"I saw them too," Yale said. "I was standing right behind you."

"I know, but—"

"I can draw them from memory."

"You can?" Lily said. "Are you sure?"

Yale started to sag, and Lily wanted to bite her bottom lip right off. "I mean, of course you can!" Lily said. "Go for it."

"How's it going, guys?" Ms. Gooch said as she stopped beside Yale.

"Great!" Lily said. "Look at the pictures Yale drew!"

Ms. Gooch gave the pictures only a glance, but she studied Lily closely. "All right," she said. "Good work."

The fact that Ms. Gooch didn't raise her eyebrows, not even one of them, made Lily feel a little better. Maybe Ms. Gooch was changing her mind about her. To make sure of it, Lily didn't argue about dancing that afternoon but went right to Leo and stood beside him.

I don't care what he does to me, she thought. *I'm going to be good and pure.*

But Leo didn't have that I'm-about-to-play-a-trick-on-you look on his face. In fact, as Ms. Gooch was finding the place on the tape, he said to her, "We learned somethin' new yesterday when you wasn't dancin'. You gotta—" and he showed her the new step.

For a minute she was suspicious. What if he was showing her the *wrong* step on purpose? But when the music finally started, it turned out to be right. She took in a deep breath and said to him, "Thanks for showing me that."

"Shad said I had to," Leo said.

That didn't keep Lily from continuing to watch her back after everybody else left to go home and she and Shad were left waiting for their next assignment from Ms. Gooch.

"IALAC," their teacher said when they were both sitting in front of her. "Do you know what that stands for?"

Shad grunted. "I Am a Lazy—"

"No," Lily cut in quickly. "It's 'I Am Lovable and Capable.' We did it last year."

"We do it every year," Ms. Gooch said, rolling her eyes. "Normally I try to get by with doing as little with it as possible because I think we have more important things to do in sixth grade. But this year, I think we need it. And you two are going to help me with it."

Shad gave an even louder grunt. "In case you ain't noticed," he said, "I ain't exactly lovable."

"Oh, but you're capable."

"Of what?"

Of making me do stupid things! Lily thought. But she kept her mouth firmly shut.

"Of working with Lily on putting up a bulletin board on that statement: I Am Lovable and Capable."

Shad shrugged. "No big deal. I put up the big stuff, and she puts up the little stuff. Where's the letters?"

Ms. Gooch leaned over and tapped Shad lightly on the temple. "Right in here," she said. "You and Lily are going to plan it. That bulletin board is all yours. I want you to create a plan."

Shad didn't seem as horrified at the idea as Lily did. As soon as Ms. Gooch went into her little office to grade papers, Lily put her face into her arms on the desktop.

"Whatsa matter with *you?*" Shad said.

"I can't do a bulletin board on 'I Am Lovable and Capable,' " she said. She lifted her head. "Because I'm not either one."

"You're kiddin' me, right?" Shad said. He snapped at the rubber band on his braces with a dirty fingernail.

"No."

"Nah, you walk around here actin' like you're that all the time."

"I might be capable of some things, but I'm definitely not lovable."

"I guess not, seein' as how your friends all dumped ya."

"You don't have to rub it in."

"Course, they ain't dissin' ya."

Lily stared at him. "They *aren't* talking about me behind my back?"

"I ain't heard 'em. Course, I don't hang around 'em or nothin'."

They aren't talking about me, Lily thought hopefully. *Maybe that's something.*

"Well, if you can't think of nothin' then I guess we take a zero or somethin'," Shad was saying. "'Cause I definitely am not lovable or whatever that other thing is."

"Capable," Lily said absently. Her mind turned from the Girlz to the problem at hand. No way she was taking a zero.

"Wake me up if you get any ideas," Shad said, and plopped his face down onto the desk.

Why do I always get stuck with these boys who can't do anything? Lily thought. *Is this some kind of punishment or something?*

And then she could almost hear Yale saying, "You never asked me."

Lily reached over and shook Shad by the arm. "Wake up," she said.

"What are we doing?"

"I don't know yet. What can you do? Can you draw?"

"No," Shad said, as if she'd just asked him if he could turn into a cockroach.

"Can you do lettering?"

This time he just shot her a look and reached for a *Scholastic* magazine that was lying on another desk. He flipped through it aimlessly while Lily gnawed at her lip.

Good grief, she thought. *His self-image is worse than mine. At least I'm trying.* And then the idea sprang into her head and waved its arms at her.

"I got it," she said. "We can put letters up there saying 'I am not lovable and capable yet, but I'm getting there.'"

"I ain't never gonna get there," Shad said. But he didn't go straight back to the magazine. "What else?" he said. "Do we gotta cut out stupid shapes or somethin'?"

Lily looked at the magazine. "Okay. We could cut out pictures from magazines of people we want to be."

"Not from *this* magazine," Shad said. "These people are geeks."

"So we'll use ones we bring in from home. We have tons."

"I guess we got some," Shad said. "But this is stupid. It's all 'what I want to be when I grow up.' That's baby stuff."

"I'm not talking when we grow up," Lily said. "More like what we want to be now."

"I'm me," Shad said. "People don't like it, they can—"

"So put up pictures of yourself, I don't care," Lily said. She could feel her neck starting to blotch. "But you just said you weren't lovable or capable."

"Nobody around here exactly loves me," Shad said. "And I don't even know what that other thing means."

"Capable?" Lily said. "It means you can do stuff. Like, you can play basketball, so you're capable of that."

"Yeah, well, tell that to that dumb coach."

"The one at your basketball camp?"

"I quit that. It was stupid." Shad shrugged about four times inside his too-big shirt. "I don't care. This whole thing is stupid."

"How stupid is staying after school for *another* week?" Ms. Gooch said from inside her office.

Chapter 11

D ude," Shad whispered. "How'd she hear that?"

"She's got ears like a bat."

Shad blinked. "Bats got ears?"

"It's more like radar," Lily said. "They have to, since they're mostly blind."

"So what do you do, sit around and read books all the time?"

"Actually, I saw that on the Discovery Channel."

"Yeah, but how'd you remember it?"

"I don't know. I just do."

"You're, like, all capable."

Lily rolled her eyes. "So do you want me to write down what we said about the bulletin board or not?"

"Yeah, I guess," Shad said.

Lily waited for him to say, "With you." But he didn't.

When Lily had finished writing down the plan, Shad yelled for Ms. Gooch. She appeared, looking a little doubtful, and took the paper from Lily. Both eyebrows went up, and Lily stifled a groan.

But Ms. Gooch smiled as she handed the paper back to Lily. "Not bad, you two," she said. "Okay, here's the deal. As soon as you put up this bulletin board and it meets my approval, you don't have to come back anymore after school. But it has to be good, and you *both* have to work on it."

"Don't worry about it," Shad said. "I'll make sure she does her share. I won't let her make me do the whole thing."

"Good," Ms. Gooch said dryly. "I'll sleep better tonight."

As for Lily, she wasn't sure she was going to sleep at all until the board was done and she could at least get away from spending every afternoon with Shad Shifferdecker.

But as she started to turn the corner from the school to go down her street—and Reni's—she stopped.

What am *I going to with my afternoons after this?* she thought. *I won't have Girlz Only Club to go to.*

She couldn't stand to think that thought, and she sure couldn't stand to walk past the clubhouse again.

She made a sharp turn and headed for the next street over. But she almost changed her mind the minute she set foot on Oakford Avenue. There about a block ahead of her was Shad, leaning against somebody's fence.

Lily squared her shoulders and decided to walk past him. Maybe since their punishment was almost over, he'd cut her some slack for a change.

But the minute he saw her, he curled up his lip and called out, "Hey, Snobbins! Come here a minute."

"What?" she said when she got to him. "And please don't say anything rude. I can't handle any more today."

"Have you seen them?"

Lily stopped talking in mid-word. "Who?"

"Who else? Daniel and Leo."

"Oh. No."

"Dude, they were supposed to wait for me right here." He looked accusingly at Lily. "They probably got sick of standin' around."

"Like that's *my* fault," Lily said.

"If you hadn't taken so long to think of a dumb idea."

"If you had even given me any help."

Lily shifted her backpack and walked on.

Again, she hadn't gone a block when she could hear him running behind her. She tried to concentrate on the tulips, the squirrels, anything. But within seconds, Shad was walking beside her, and then there was no concentrating on anything else.

"So how come you can't handle me talkin' trash to ya? I thought you had, like, brothers."

"I do," Lily said coldly.

"Are they pansies or something?"

"*What*?"

"Are they, like, too chicken to say anything to ya?"

"No! They're rude too. All boys are rude! Now would you just leave me alone?"

"No," Shad said. "I like buggin' you."

Boy, Mrs. Cavanaugh was sure wrong about this one, Lily thought miserably. *He doesn't* like *me—he just likes making me suffer!*

"You wanna know why?" Shad said.

"No," Lily said.

"It's because I want to take you down. You're so stuck-up."

Lily had to stop then, only she couldn't stop her mouth. "I am *not* stuck-up!" she said to him. "To be stuck-up, you have to be conceited, and I'm not conceited! I *hate* myself!"

"Nuh-unh," Shad said. "You love yourself. You think you're . . . "

But he didn't have a chance to finish. A small body flew around the corner just ahead of them and careened to a stop in Shad's path. He was red-faced and wheezing, and it took Lily a minute to realize it was Yale.

"Shad!" Yale's voice was high-pitched and quivering, and he was definitely having trouble breathing. In fact, he fumbled into his pocket and took out what Lily recognized as an asthma inhaler. She'd seen one of the girls on her mother's volleyball team use one a couple of times. But Yale didn't put it to his mouth; he just held it in his hand, which he waved around as he said, "Leo and Daniel—they need your help!"

"For what?" Shad said, eyes narrowing.

"I don't know! They're down by the river. They just said for you to come—quick—they're in some kinda trouble!"

It was the most Lily had ever heard Yale say, and it must have been a little too much because he put the inhaler up to his mouth and puffed away.

"What kinda trouble?" Shad said.

Yale shrugged. Shad took off at a run.

"Is somebody hurt?" Lily said to Yale.

Yale took the inhaler out and said, "I don't know. She didn't tell me that part." Lily hiked her backpack firmly onto her shoulders and took off after Shad.

At the top of the wall that ran along the Delaware River, she could already hear Shad shouting, and there was something in his voice she hadn't heard from him before.

"Leo!" he was calling out. "Daniel!"

It was a lot like the voice her mother had used one time when Joe had gotten separated from them on the Boardwalk in Atlantic City.

When Lily got to the river wall, Shad was pacing around like a confused duck. Leo and Daniel were nowhere to be seen.

"What's goin' on?" Shad said.

"Like I know," Lily said. "Maybe they're hiding from you."

Shad shook his head and pointed down. Lily followed his finger to two bicycles on the ground at the edge of the wall.

"If they were hidin', why would they leave their bikes right out here?"

"Those are theirs?" Lily said. "Are you sure?"

"What do you think, I'm stupid? I ride with 'em everyday. These are, like, way expensive bikes. Nobody else has 'em at our school."

Lily got an uneasy feeling in her stomach. The bikes looked as if they'd been tossed there, and not very carefully. Why would Leo and Daniel leave "way expensive bikes" out here for somebody to steal?

"Leo!" Shad shouted again. "Daniel!"

The anxious sound of his voice pulled Lily's stomach into a knot. "Let's look for them," she said. "I'll go that way. You go down there."

Shad nodded like he was numb and bolted off, still yelling his friends' names. He was sounding more and more scared with every yell.

Maybe we just ought to tell a grown-up, Lily thought as she hurried up along the river, scanning the park with her hand shielding her eyes from the sun. There weren't that many trees, so you could see quite a ways. If the two boys were hiding, they were sure good at it. And they'd have to be completely deaf not to hear Shad squalling their names.

Lily looked behind the snack stand, which wasn't open for the season yet, and in back of the band shell and even between the cars parked along the street. No Daniel, and no Leo.

Shad's shouting was sounding frantic by then, so Lily ran back to the bikes. Sweat glistened on the scalp you could see beneath his almost-shaved hair. He was pacing again and flinging his arms around like he didn't know what to do with them.

"I think we better tell somebody they're missing," Lily said.

"They wouldn't do somethin' stupid, like get in somebody's car with 'em," Shad said. "Do ya think?"

Lily shook her head. "No, but maybe they got scared by something and ran."

"Me and Leo and Daniel don't *get* scared," Shad said.

"Then maybe they were chasing somebody else."

"They'd of done it on their bikes. You don't understand—I *know* them."

A pang went through Lily. *You're lucky, Shad,* she wanted to say. *At least you still* have *your friends.*

91

Shad stood at the edge of the wall, looking down at the river. "They wouldn't of jumped."

"Uh, no! Even *boys* aren't *that* stupid. That water's deep, and it's dirty. Gross!"

"What if they fell?"

"I don't think—"

"What if somebody pushed 'em?" He darted his eyes to Lily.

"What are you looking at me for? I wasn't even here!"

Shad suddenly tore off his sweatshirt and yanked his T-shirt off with it. His bare flesh broke out into gooseflesh in the brisk spring wind coming off the river.

"Why are you taking off your clothes?" Lily said.

"I'm goin' in after 'em."

"In *there?*"

Shad didn't answer but kicked his Timberlands out of the way and made for the edge of the wall.

"No, don't jump!" Lily cried. But Shad bent his legs and swung back his arms, poised to hurl himself right into the river.

"Don't!" Lily cried out again.

She lunged for him, grabbing him by his right arm. He tried to yank it away, but Lily held on.

Seconds later, they had both left the wall and were tumbling through the air toward the Delaware River.

Chapter 12

Lily had been right. The water was deep, and it was dirty. Her feet didn't touch the bottom, and the mouthful she swallowed tasted like greasy socks. She came up choking.

But what she *hadn't* known was that it would be so cold. Its chill against her skin took her breath away.

Shad didn't appear to be breathing any too well himself. A few feet away from her, he was coughing and sputtering like a dying boat motor, which was no surprise, seeing how his head kept disappearing beneath the surface.

"Shad!" Lily hollered to him. "Are you okay?"

There was no answer, just more burbling and splashing as his hands flailed in the water.

"Shad?" she said. She paddled closer. "Can't you swim?"

Shad flung out an arm and caught Lily by the sweater sleeve. Before she could even shout at him again, he had yanked her under the water.

Lily fought her way to the top, with Shad still holding tight to her sweater. His other hand caught her by the front of her blouse, and she could feel herself going under again. Without even thinking about it, Lily pulled up a leg and gave him a sharp kick in the stomach. He let go of her and sank.

Free now, Lily swam the three strokes it took to get to the wall and clung to it as she smeared the water out of her eyes.

"That wasn't *funny,* Shad!" she screamed. "You could drown somebody that way."

Shad answered by throwing his hands around and coughing. He choked out a weak, panicky "Help!"

Then his head went under again, but it was slower coming up this time. And this time, she was the one who yelled, "Help!"

Shad stopped flailing with his arms. His head disappeared once more, and it didn't bob back up. Beneath the murky water, she could see his eyes bulging in terror.

Terrified herself, Lily swam back out to him. She was so cold by now her teeth were clacking against each other and her arms and legs didn't want to move. She managed to get herself to him, only this time he didn't try to grab her. She grabbed *him* by the arm and swam as hard as she could with her now almost-numb legs toward the wall again.

As soon as her hand touched it, she braced herself up against it and reached out and pulled Shad's head up. He coughed—hard—and then threw up into the water.

"*Help!*" Lily screamed. "Somebody help! He's drowning for real!"

"Hang on, honey!" somebody yelled from above. "Just hang on and keep his head up!"

"Hurry!" she cried. Shad was like a lead weight in her hands now, and she could feel herself slipping against the side of the wall.

"I'm coming, honey! Hold on!"

She closed her eyes and prayed, and just as the faceless voice had promised, someone came and fastened a belt around her. Someone else pulled her up out of the water and back to the top of the wall. A man in a uniform picked her up and carried her to a grassy spot.

"You okay?" he said.

"Shad was drowning! Did somebody get him?"

"Where is he? Where's Shad?"

Lily recognized Leo's and Daniel's voices. They were obviously as scared as she felt.

"Kid!" Lily's policeman yelled. "Get me a blanket out of the patrol car."

But Leo said, "That's Shad," and two pairs of footsteps pounded toward the wall.

The policeman himself got Lily wrapped up in a blanket, and when he was sure she wasn't hurt, he sat her up. She could see two paramedics working on Shad. Where they had come from she had no idea. The whole thing felt like one of those dreams where people drift in and out of nowhere and nobody else seems to think it's weird.

But when Shad threw up again and fought two paramedics and a policeman so he could sit up, Lily was glad they were all there, real or not.

"Is he gonna be okay?" Lily asked her policeman.

The officer grinned. "Oh, I think he's gonna be fine—until his daddy gets a hold of him for playing around the river."

Lily watched Shad, who was trying to talk to Leo and Daniel while the paramedics took his blood pressure and shined a little flashlight in his eyes.

What's going on? She thought. *Where were they when Shad got here?*

And then suddenly, Lily felt very, very tired, and she sagged back down onto the grass. "Can I just go home now?"

"As soon as the paramedics have a look at you. Why don't you tell me your phone number, and I'll contact your parents?"

Oh no, Lily thought. *Now I'm gonna be grounded for the rest of my life!*

As it turned out, it wasn't quite that bad. Dad came and took her home and told her to take a hot bath. Mom got there right after that, her face white and pinched the way it almost never looked unless somebody was running a temperature of more than 103.

"What on *earth*, Lil?" Mom said. "What were you doing at the river in the first place? Are you losing your marbles, girl!"

Dad stopped Mom with a hand on her arm. Lily didn't even look up to catch the conversation they were having over her head. She waited, shivering in her towel, until Mom said, "Get dressed, and I'll make you some cocoa."

Lily changed, and she sat on the couch and drank dutifully, even though the cocoa tasted remarkably like the river water to her. While Mom and Dad sat on the coffee table facing her and listened with their whole faces, Lily told them the story.

"So you still don't know where Leo and Daniel were all that time?" Mom said.

"No."

Mom sniffed. "That Shifferdecker boy isn't playing with a full deck as far as I can see. Why would he assume they'd fallen into the water and dive in there after them when he obviously can't even swim?"

"It's quite ironic, when you think about it," Dad said.

"Ironic?" Lily said. "Is that bad?"

"Not in this case. You had to save the life of a boy you can hardly stand."

Lily stared at her father. "I couldn't just let him drown, Daddy!" she said. "He's a person!"

"I'm glad to see he's risen on the food chain," Mom said.

"You know something, Lilliputian?" Dad said.

Lily shook her wet head.

"I think you're making some progress. You thought a lot less about yourself down there than you did about Chad's self—"

"Shad."

"Shad?" Dad looked momentarily bewildered. "Who would name a poor child Shad?"

"You were making a point, dear," Mom said.

"I was. Right." Dad focused his blue eyes back onto Lily. "What I have been trying to get you to see from the Bible verses I've given you is that your image of other people is so much more important than your image of yourself. It's all about love for God and for your fellow human being, no matter what he's done to you."

"I do *not* love Shad Shifferdecker!" Lily said.

"We're not talking about the kissy-face, huggy-bear kind of love," Mom said. "This is love for a person because he's one of God's own."

"Where are my glasses?" Dad said.

He patted his shirt pocket and squinted around the room. Mom pulled his specs down from on top of his head and placed them on his face.

"Hand me that Bible, would you?" he said.

"Do you see why men get married?" Mom said to Lily as she reached for the Bible on the end table. "They need women to hold them together, or they would fall completely apart. Although I think having to dive into the Delaware to fish the man out is a bit extreme."

"All right, listen to this," Dad said. He cleared his throat and read, "'Love the Lord your God with all your heart and with all your soul and with all your mind. This is the first and greatest commandment. And the second is like it: Love your neighbor as yourself.'" Dad looked at Lily over the top of his glasses. "There are three parts to these commandments. Love God. Love your neighbor. Love yourself. Only one-third of that is about yourself—your self-image. The other two are intertwined with that." He laced his fingers together. "You can't do one without the others. Perhaps, Lilliputian, this little incident today is telling you to concentrate on how you look at *other* people. What are you willing to do for them? That shows you what kind of a self you have."

Mom picked up one of Lily's still-cold feet and rubbed it between her hands. "Did it ever occur to you today not to try to save Shad—to just let him go ahead and drown?"

"No!" Lily said.

"And have you told on any of the other people who were involved in the glue fiasco?"

"No," Lily said. And then she could feel her face blotching. "Except I never said that anybody else was involved in it."

"You didn't have to. But that's the point—you could have hauled them all down with you, and you didn't. You are a much better person than you think you are, but you still need to work on how you look at other people."

"Like Yale," Lily said.

"Yale?" Dad said. "Where *do* these parents get these names?"

"Personally, Lil," Mom said, "I think you ought to leave your self alone. You're doing just fine in spite of yourself."

Lily could feel her throat starting to close up, and she knew she'd better say something before she started to cry. "You guys are the best," she said.

Dad looked at Mom. "We are, aren't we?"

"I think so," Mom said. Then she gave one of her rare smiles. "Nothing wrong with *our* self-image!"

Lily stood up and hugged them both and then headed for the door.

"Where are you going?" Dad said.

"To my room."

"Lil," Mom said. "Groundation is over. I think we've made our point."

That, at least, was a good thing. Lily liked being able to do her homework in the family room that night instead of being confined to her bedroom, alone with a self she still didn't like very much.

But there was still something sad about it. It didn't do her much good to be able to use the phone, especially since her friends had dumped her.

She did get a phone call that night though. But it wasn't from any of the Girlz. It was from Shad. This time, he identified himself.

"This is Shad," he said gruffly.

"Are you okay?" Lily said.

"Yeah. I'm still coughin' up junk." To prove it, he hawked back a particularly unattractive loogey and spat into what Lily hoped was a nearby trash can. She rolled her eyes as she waited.

"Anyways," he said, "you gotta talk to that Yale kid for me."

"Why?" Lily said.

"'Cause Leo an' Daniel said *he* was the one told *them* that I was in trouble down at the river. That's why they went down there in the first place."

"Then I don't get it," Lily said.

"Neither do I. Nobody does. That's why you gotta ask the little creep what was up with it."

"Why me? Why don't you ask him?"

"'Cause I want to pound him, and, if I get in any more trouble for fightin', I'll, like, fail the sixth grade or somethin'."

"I could try, I guess," Lily said. "Is that all you wanted?"

"Yeah. Oh no, I guess thanks for savin' me from drownin'."

"Sure," Lily said.

"Okay, well, bye," Shad said.

"Bye," Lily said, and then she remembered something. "Hey, Shad," she said.

"What?"

"Where did Leo and Daniel go? How come they didn't hear you yelling for them?"

"They were chasing somebody that dropped water balloons out of a tree on 'em. And get this, they were filled with red Kool-Aid. Daniel's mom is, like, ready to put him up for adoption or somethin' 'cause it messed up his shirt. I gotta go."

99

Lily nodded and hung up the phone. She even forgot to remind him to bring his stuff for the bulletin board tomorrow.

All she could think about was water balloons filled with red Kool-Aid.

It couldn't be, could it?

There was only one way to find out, and that was to ask Yale—if he knew. When she'd asked him just that day, was anybody hurt, he'd said, "I don't know. She didn't tell me."

Lily stared down at the phone. She? Who was "she"?

Once again, there was only one way to find out.

Chapter 13

The next morning before school, Shad tossed a big brown envelope on Lily's desk and said, "Keep this, or I'll lose it. My mother says I lose stuff because I'm male."

Lily tried not to look suspicious. She really was trying to have a better image of other people. Still, with Shad, it was hard. She couldn't help wondering as she stared at the envelope whether whatever was in it was alive or slimy or both.

When she didn't pick it up, Shad said, "It's that stuff for that dumb bulletin board."

"It's magazines?"

"No, it's pictures. My old lady grounded me last night, and since I didn't have nothin' else to do, I cut out a bunch of stuff."

Shad started to move on and then stopped. After looking over both shoulders, he whispered hoarsely, "Don't forget what you gotta do today—you know—talk to—"

He jerked his head in Yale's direction.

Lily nodded, and when Shad finally slouched off to his seat, Lily put the envelope under her desk. She didn't have time to look inside it right away. For one thing, she was afraid to. There was no telling what Shad had cut out to represent the person he wanted to be. WWF wrestlers came to mind, and so did skaters with lots of chains hanging from their britches.

Lily turned her thoughts to questioning Yale. The problem was, Lily wasn't so sure she really wanted to know. Every time she thought about Yale saying, "I don't know. She didn't tell me," and every time the water balloons filled with red Kool-Aid crossed Lily's mind, so did Reni.

When they were finally working on their projects, Shad gave his head a jerk toward Yale that was so sharp, Lily was sure he was going to have to go straight to the chiropractor after school.

"All *right!*" she mouthed to him and turned to Yale.

"Yale," she said, "we need to talk." She'd seen that done on TV, and it always got people to sit down and discuss things. It got Yale inspecting his shoelaces with unblinking eyes.

Lily plowed on. "I need you to tell me who told you to tell Shad that Leo and Daniel were in trouble at the river."

"I don't remember," he said to the toe of his sneaker.

"Who told you to tell Leo and Daniel that Shad was in trouble at the river first?"

"I don't remember that either."

"I bet you do," Lily said. "You just don't want to tell me."

"I *can't* tell you!"

Yale's voice rose up to a pitch that out whined Zooey's, and he raced for the classroom door.

Lily hurried across the classroom.

"Yale's upset," she said to Ms. Gooch. "Can I go find him?"

"Uh, yes, and bring him back here. You people are not free to come and go as you please!"

Lily found Yale just ready to plunge into the boys' bathroom. She grabbed his arm before he could go inside.

"It's okay, Yale," she said to him.

Yale snatched his skinny arm away, but he didn't make a dive for the door. "It's not okay," he said. "Shad and those guys are gonna pound me now. They keep on lookin' at me."

"They're not going to get *you*," Lily said. "They're going to get *them.*"

"Who?"

"Whoever put you up to it."

Yale's face turned even paler if that were possible. "You don't want that!" he said. "Trust me, you don't!"

Lily felt her own skin draining of color. "It was Reni, wasn't it?" she said.

"She didn't tell me it was gonna go that far! She didn't tell me people were gonna almost drown! I just wanted somebody to like me for a change, and I figured if I helped—"

Yale couldn't even finish the sentence. He sagged against the brick wall and crumpled his face as if he were squeezing back tears.

"I don't get it," Lily said. "You wanted to help play a trick on Shad and those guys so they would *like* you?"

"I didn't know it was a trick at first! They just wanted me to give Leo and Daniel a message, and I figured if I could talk to 'em just one time without 'em makin' fun of me, that would at least be *somethin'.*" Yale kicked the toe of one sneaker with the heel of the other. "Then when they told me to give Shad the same message, it was too late to back out. And they were bein' nice to me—"

Another light popped on in Lily's head. "They?" she said. "Who's they?"

"All your friends," he said. "I figured girls bein' nice to me was better'n nobody at all."

He really did start to cry then, and Lily wasn't sure what to do. If it had been one of the Girlz, she would have thrown her arms around her. But this was Yale. He was so—

So what? she thought suddenly. *Stupid and geeky and doesn't have any friends?*

That was what Yale thought of him*self,* which was plain. But what was *her* image of him, like Dad had told her to think about?

"You know something, Yale?" Lily said. "You don't need Shad and Leo and Daniel to have friends. You could have plenty of friends if people knew you were, like, this artist and that you do things for people when they want help." She heard her own voice getting fierce, and she even put her hands on her hips. "You should let other people get to know you like I do, and then you wouldn't have to be alone."

Yale glanced up at her for a second and smeared the back of his hands across his eyes. "I'm gonna go," he nodded toward the bathroom, "y'know."

When he had disappeared inside, Lily sagged against the wall. She didn't want to go back to the classroom, where Ms. Gooch was going to raise her eyebrows at her and Shad was going to want to know what she'd been able to "pound out of" Yale.

I know just how you feel, Yale, she thought. *I'm all alone too.*

As she pulled herself away from the wall and went slowly back toward the classroom, she wished her aloneness was as easy to solve as Yale's. But although Reni looked up when Lily walked into the classroom, she quickly turned her head away. Zooey was so intent on erasing something she was making a hole in her paper, and Suzy had her whole face buried in a book. Only Kresha started to smile at Lily, and then it was as if she'd just remembered a stomachache and lapsed into an uncomfortable frown.

"Let's go to lunch, people," Ms. Gooch said.

"Meet me by the bike racks after lunch!" Shad hissed to her as the class pushed through the doorway.

"Why?" she whispered back.

"You know why!"

She did. But she knew what it meant. And even though Reni and Kresha and Suzy and Zooey had let her take the whole punishment for the glue caper all by herself, and even though their trick on Shad and Leo and Daniel almost ended in something *really* awful, Lily didn't want to tell on them.

I don't know why not, she thought, as she watched Reni lead the way across the playground to the tree where Lily used to gather with them. *I should just let them take what they have coming to them from Shad and those guys. Why should I try to protect them? They didn't help me when I needed it.*

But as she took her last, draggy steps toward the bike racks where Shad was sprawled on top like a king lounging on his throne, Lily knew why. Because she wasn't like that. When she got rid of the evil thoughts and made room for God, that wasn't how she saw herself.

And that wasn't the way she saw her Girlz, either. They were being mean to her right now, but they didn't deserve to have Shad coming after them, no matter what.

She stopped several feet from the bike rack.

"So come here," Shad said.

"I'm fine here," Lily said. "I just came to tell you what I found out."

Shad's lip curled practically up to his nostrils. "Don't be yellin' it from out there! Come 'ere!"

"There's nothing to yell," Lily said. "Yale didn't know the people. He can't help you." Then she added quickly. "He wants to—he really does. He's a nice kid."

"He's a sis," Leo said.

"How would you know?" Lily said. "You don't even know him."

"You don't either," Daniel said.

"Yes, I do."

"So, is he your boyfriend now?"

Lily bit her lip to keep from continuing the conversation. She looked at Shad. He had his eyes so narrowed they appeared to be about to collide at the nose.

"What if I go pound him?" Shad said. "Will he tell me?"

"How could he tell you? He doesn't know the people!"

That was pretty much true. He didn't really *know* the Girlz.

"Man, I wanna know who tried to make fools of us!" Daniel said.

"They didn't try—they *did*," Shad said. "That's even worse."

"Well, y'know, nobody told you to jump in the river," Leo said.

"And nobody told you to open your mouth just now, either," Shad snapped back. "How 'bout if I just pound *you*!"

Lily was sure he would have, right there before her eyes, if Shad hadn't suddenly sat up straight on the bike rack and shifted his eyes.

"What?" Leo said.

Shad put his finger to his lips and pointed to the wall just beyond them that hid a dumpster from public view.

"Is somebody back there?" Daniel whispered.

Shad gave him another *shhh* and tiptoed toward the wall. Even as he did, something metal crashed and rolled, as if somebody had tripped over a trash can and knocked it over.

"Get 'em!" Shad shouted.

The three of them took off in pursuit of whoever had been unlucky enough to be listening from behind that wall. Lily hoped it wasn't poor Yale.

But as she walked listlessly back out to the playground, she spotted Yale perched on a swing, busily racing his pencil over a notebook. That was a relief anyway.

Lily wandered around a little—picked up some trash—avoided Ashley and her friends—asked the teacher on duty what time it was. Finally she couldn't think of anything else to do to keep from just sitting down and bawling, so she asked if she could go inside and use the restroom.

It wasn't much weirder being in the hall whenever everyone was outside, Lily decided, than it was for her any other time these days. She was always just by herself. Period.

But when she pulled open the bathroom door, it was apparent that there *was* someone else in there. It was Kresha, leaning over the sink, breathing like she'd just run a marathon. Her usually pale face was bright red, and her hair was sticking out in all directions—even more so than usual.

"Oh," Lily said. "Are you all right?"

"Hi, Lee-lee," Kresha said.

Her voiced sounded sad. Lily took another step toward her.

"What's wrong?" Lily said. "Did you get hurt?"

"No."

"Are you sick?"

"No, not sick."

"Are you upset?"

"No, not set up. Just—you know—" She tilted her head to the side and pulled the corners of her mouth down with her fingers.

"Sad," Lily said.

"Yah."

Lily went over to the sink and tried to get some soap to come out of the soap dispenser that never worked. Her mind was spinning. It was the first time any of them had even spoken to her since the day *it* had happened, and it felt inside out to be talking as if nothing had ever happened.

"Lee-lee?" Kresha said.

"Huh?"

"Yale—he do know us. You lie."

Lily jerked her head up. Kresha was wiping the sweat off of her forehead with a wet paper towel and watching Lily closely.

She shrugged.

"I miss you, Lee-lee," Kresha said.

And then she bolted out of the bathroom before Lily could say a word. As the door sighed shut, Lily whispered, "I miss you too. All of you."

Chapter 14

The school day finally ground to a halt, and there was only the bulletin board to do before Lily could go home. At least at her house, people talked to her. Well, some people. There was still Joe.

How did everything get so messed up all at once? she thought sadly.

"All right, you two, remember our deal," Ms. Gooch said when the rest of the class had finally left for good. "You finish the bulletin board today, and I will commute your sentence."

"What does that mean?" Lily said.

"Means we get out early for good behavior," Shad said.

"Shad, I hope it's not experience that makes you so familiar with that word," Ms. Gooch said, half-smiling at him.

"I ain't never been arrested or nothin', if that's what you mean," Shad said. "My old lady has me on a leash. I gotta ask permission to go to the bathroom."

"That was a little more information than I wanted to hear," Ms. Gooch said. "But thanks for sharing. Get to work."

While Shad collected a stapler and some construction paper from Ms. Gooch, Lily settled herself at a table and arranged the pictures she'd spent afternoon recess cutting out while sitting on the edge of a basketball court nobody was using. Ever since Shad had quit basketball camp, Lily hadn't seen him dribbling imaginary balls everywhere and trying to jump as high as the hoop all through recess.

"Did you look at my pictures?" he said now as he pulled back the open stapler like a hammer and nailed a staple into the bulletin board.

"No," Lily said. "Is it a bunch of basketball players?"

"Nah—basketball's lame."

He went back to attaching pieces of construction paper to the board with mighty karate thrusts of the stapler, complete with sound effects, leg kicks, and elaborate bows.

He was *so* weird. But not quite as weird as Lily had expected. The pictures that slid from the envelope surprised her.

There were none of skaters with words shaved in their hair or of championship wrestlers wearing silk boxers. The only one that showed anything even close to violence was a guy in a karate uniform, and he was concentrating on breaking a pile of cinder blocks with the side of his hand. The rest of the pictures had Lily's mouth gaping open.

One showed a handsome, warm-looking man sitting in a big, comfortable chair reading a book to a little boy.

Another was a picture of a whole family sitting at a table about to dig into an extra-large pizza.

The third was of a teenage guy sitting on the hood of a car with a bunch of other guys and girls all around him, looking at him as if he'd just said something hilarious that had them all in stitches and waiting for his next line.

"You're doing that creepy thing again," Shad said.

He jumped down from the chair he'd been standing on and closed up the stapler as if he were snapping a switchblade shut. Lily hadn't even been aware that she'd been staring at him.

"This is the person you want to be?" Lily asked.

"Yeah," Shad said, curling his lip. "You got a problem with that?"

"I guess not—but what do they mean?"

Shad put down the stapler and snatched the pictures from her. "A really decent dad—since my old man ran out on me when I was, like, two. The head of a family with actual people in it, not just, like, one parent and one kid so you never get to order the biggest-size pizza." He grinned at the third one. "And the most popular guy on the planet."

"What about this one?" Lily said, pointing to the karate photo.

"I wanna be a black belt."

"Why? So you can pound people like Yale?"

"You don't 'pound' people in karate," Shad said, eyes squinted in contempt. "It's like this disciplined art thing. You wouldn't get it."

Lily shrugged.

"Besides," Shad said, "I don't gotta pound the little wimp 'cause I *know* who tried to pull that trick yesterday."

"No, you do not!"

"You sounded just like her just then."

Lily half rose from her chair. "Shad Shifferdecker, you leave Reni alone! And the other girls too. They didn't mean for it to go that far, I know they didn't! Nobody told you to jump in the river when you can't even swim!"

"So it *was* them! Gotcha!"

"Leave them alone!"

Shad shook his head at her. "Dude—I don't get you. You'd think you'd want to get back at them after the way they ditched you."

"What if it was Leo and Daniel who ditched you?" Lily said. "Would you just turn around and hate them?"

"My friends wouldn't ever do that though."

Lily stopped and sank back into the seat. "I didn't think mine would, either."

Shad didn't answer that time. He just ambled over to the bulletin board and held up a picture.

"I don't know where to put these," he said. "Let me see yours first."

She shrugged and pushed her pile of pictures toward him. He looked at the array of women smiling and laughing and hugging people and gave a grunt.

"I don't care if you like them or not," Lily said. "You got to pick yours, and I got to pick mine and—"

"Why you gotta jump on everything I say? I didn't say I didn't like 'em. I just thought you'd come in with all these women bossin' people around in big companies or somethin'."

"That's not who I want to be," Lily said. And she added sadly to herself, *I just want to have people liking me again.*

It took a while to get the letters right so they weren't crooked or didn't run downhill. Shad said he didn't want something dumb up there where everybody knew he did it. Lily had to admit she didn't either.

Once the board read I AM NOT LOVABLE AND CAPABLE YET, BUT I'M GETTING THERE, they changed their minds at least eighteen times apiece about the best way to place the pictures. At first it seemed like Lily should have her side and Shad should have his, but it looked better with the pictures all mixed in together. Better balance, Lily said.

"I don't know," Shad said. "It just doesn't look as dumb."

Once it was altogether, they stood back as far as they could and looked at it. Lily was surprised at how good it looked. Even Shad gave one of his less obnoxious grunts.

"Hey, Ms. Gooch!" he called out. "Come see what we done."

Ms. Gooch joined them from her office and stood beside them. It made Lily a little nervous when the teacher stood there for several minutes, frowning at their masterpiece.

"Is there somethin' wrong with it?" Shad said finally.

"Oh no, it's lovely." Ms. Gooch gave Lily a sideways glance. "As I knew it would be." She turned to Shad. "Tell me, Shad. Which one of you cut out all the pictures?"

"We both done 'em!" Shad said. "She cut out hers, and I cut out mine!"

"Is that right, Lily?" Ms. Gooch said.

"Why you gotta ask her?" Shad said.

"Shad, when have you ever done something yourself when you could get someone else to do it for you?"

"I didn't do it for him," Lily said. "We each cut out our own pictures. And he had his done first."

Ms. Gooch stepped closer to the board and looked at it some more. Shad made a face behind her back. Lily went nervously up to her.

"Honest, Ms. Gooch," she said. "Shad did just as much work as I did."

"Did you look at his pictures first before you chose yours?"

"You sayin' she cheated or somethin'?" Shad said.

"No, but I know what a perfectionist Lily is."

"I'm not perfect!" Lily said. "I never said that!"

Ms. Gooch put her hand on Lily's arm. "Calm down, girl," she said. "I didn't say you were perfect, I said you *try* to be and you're never satisfied until you are. My point is—those pictures are so beautifully coordinated, it looks like one person chose them—or like you're describing two people who are very much alike." Her face broke into a smile. "And we know *that* isn't true!" She laughed, even though Lily and Shad didn't laugh with her, and said, "Okay—nice job, guys. Now both of you get out of here, and I don't want to have to hang out after school with either one of you ever again."

"You won't," Lily said.

Ms. Gooch looked at Shad. "Are you going to make me the same promise?"

Shad shrugged. When Ms. Gooch had gone back into her office, he scowled at Lily. "So I guess I'm not perfect like you. She expects me to get in trouble, so I might as well just do it anyway."

"Her image of you is wrong," Lily said.

"You sound like that shrink my old lady made me go to one time."

"Whatever," Lily said.

Shad shrugged again, and then he did something that made Lily stare at him harder than ever. He stuck out his hand to her.

She didn't ask him what he thought he was doing. She didn't peek into it for possible buzzers. She just stuck hers out too, and they shook hands.

"I ain't gonna mess with your friends," he said.

"Why?" she said.

"'Cause you didn't let Ms. Gooch diss me."

"Oh," Lily said.

"But don't expect me to, like, eat lunch with you or nothin'."

"No way!"

"All right."

"All right."

Then they both got their backpacks and went their separate ways toward home. Lily was so lost in thought, she forgot to take a detour, and before she knew it, she was in front of Reni's house. She couldn't help it—she stopped and listened for the sounds of their voices.

But the clubhouse was quiet. Not the kind of quiet from four girls whispering their plans, but a dead kind of quiet, as if there weren't any girls there anymore.

They probably went out to get Baskin Robbins or something, Lily thought.

It was warm enough for that now—and for sitting outside and painting each other's toenails and putting suntan lotion on each other's backs—and then in a couple of weeks they would be planning all the cool stuff they were going to do together when school was out.

Lily took a big, shuddering breath. *I know that's what they'll be doing,* she thought. *I know them!* If only they would give her a chance to tell them that.

Already digging into her backpack for a piece of paper and a pencil, she headed across the Johnsons' perfect lawn to the clubhouse. She had been right. There was no one there. The pillows were scattered all over, and there were candy wrappers on the floor, and somebody had even left the power on the tape deck turned on. Mrs. Johnson must not have been out there lately.

Lily tidied up a little, just so she would have a place to sit down and write. But when she finally got settled, it was hard to start. All she could do was sit there and *feel* the Girlz all around her.

She could smell Zooey's snacks—the squeeze cheeses and the hunks of salami.

She could see Kresha's footprints—the ones she'd made before Lily had told her the Girlz *did not* prop their dirty feet on the wall.

She could practically hear Suzy's nervous giggle floating in the air.

And she could almost feel Reni, nudging her every time Kresha said something funny or Zooey said she was hungry for the forty-fifth time.

Lily *did* know them, and that was what she had to tell them. That it didn't matter what they thought of themselves right now—*she* knew they were wonderful, and, if they would have her, she wanted to be back with them.

She wrote until her hand got sore and she had to shake it out, and then she wrote some more. Then she folded the note neatly and put it on top of the tidy stack of pillows she'd formed so they would see it the minute they came back.

For just a moment after she stepped outside and clicked the door shut behind her, Lily had an urge to go right back in and tear it up.

What if they have decided it's better without me after all? she thought. *What if I'm all wrong about them? What if I end up feeling like an idiot?*

But she left the note there anyway. And when she did, her mind felt wide-open—at least for a few minutes. On her way home, she even splashed her toes in a couple of luscious-looking puddles.

But that feeling disappeared when she got home and discovered Joe at the kitchen table doing his homework and devouring an entire bag of Doritos.

"Where's Mom?" she said.

He shrugged and chewed with bulging cheeks.

"Yes, you do too know," Lily said. "She wouldn't leave you by yourself and not tell you where she was."

Joe took out the chip he'd just deposited into his mouth, said, "She went to the bank. She'll be back in five," and stuffed the Dorito back in. Then he arched himself over his homework and ignored her.

The silence was more than she could stand—even from Joe.

"Are you ever going to talk to me again?" she said.

He shook his head.

"Not even if I tell you I'm sorry I made you mess up at the basketball camp that day?"

"No."

"Not even if I mean it?"

"You don't."

"Yes, I do!"

He obviously wasn't buying it. Lily got out some salsa and put it in a bowl and set it on the table. Joe looked longingly at it, but he deliberately chomped down on a naked chip.

"Would you stop being mad at me if I told you I think you were the best player out there, even better than the fifth and sixth graders?"

"You are such a liar!"

"I am not! Mom and Dad say you're a natural athlete."

Joe looked at her before thrusting a hand back into the bag. "I already know that. I don't need you to tell me."

"You're also the best looking one in our family."

"Who cares?"

"I would love to be good looking! I would also love to be an athlete—or a musician—or a something!"

116

She knew her face was getting blotchy. Before Joe could start yakking about her having a skin disease, she turned to go.

"You really think I'm good-looking?" Joe said.

"Yes. Your hair's all smooth instead of sticking out all over like mine. You have Mom's eyes so nobody ever says you look at them weird. You've got—"

"Who cares?" Joe said.

But from the way his doe eyes were shining, Lily knew he did.

"How come you're sayin' all this stuff?" Joe said.

"Because I wanted to tell you my image of you."

"You're weird."

"Is that your image of me?" Lily said.

"I guess so, whatever that is."

It was enough for now. Lily felt somehow better as she went for the door again.

"Hey," Joe said.

"What?"

"You aren't all *that* ugly."

Lily went to her room feeling a whole lot better. When she tossed her backpack onto the bed, it fell on top of the Bible she'd left spread out there. She rescued it and looked again at the thing from Matthew Dad had told her to study.

I definitely love God, she thought. *I'm trying to be pure and make room. And I've really been working on loving my neighbor.*

She rolled her eyes. Those had been some tough cases.

But was she going to be able to love herself again? She'd been doing her homework at her desk for a good fifteen minutes before it came to her.

I'm sitting in here by myself when I don't have to be! I guess I don't hate myself that much anymore.

She sure hoped there were four Girlz who didn't either.

Chapter 15

By the time Lily got to school the next morning, a bunch of kids had already gathered around the bulletin board.

Actually, it was Shad they were gathered around as he pointed out every detail of every picture while they all listened. It looked like part of his dream was coming true already.

"What about the girl stuff?" Ashley was saying. "Did you do that part too?"

"Nah, that was Snobbins," Shad said. "She can tell you about that part—but it's, like, the same thing."

Shad gave his head a jerk, as if he wanted Lily to join him at the bulletin board. But Ms. Gooch called her name from the doorway.

"Could you join us out here in the hall, please?" she said.

Lily stopped like a lead weight when she got out to the hall and found Ms. Gooch with Kresha, Suzy, Zooey, and Reni. They were all looking down at the floor as if someone had dropped a contact lens.

"The girls here have just told me an interesting story," Ms. Gooch said. "They tell me they were all in on the glue incident with you. Is that true?"

Lily chewed at her lip. She had been hoping, praying for this, for so long. Now that it was happening, she didn't know what to say.

This wasn't what I was asking you to do in my note! Lily wanted to cry out at them. *You didn't have to do this! I didn't ask you to—*

"Should I take that as a yes, Lily?" Ms. Gooch said.

Lily swallowed. She chewed her lip some more. Finally, she chanced a glance at the Girlz. Zooey and Suzy were still staring miserably at the floor. But Kresha was smiling at her—smiling and whispering, "Lee-lee—it's okay, Lee-lee."

And Reni—Reni had big tears ready to splash right out of her eyes.

"They always tell the truth. I know that about them," Lily said. "Do you really need me to say it? If they told you, it must be true."

"They may always tell the truth," Ms. Gooch said dryly. "It just takes them a long time to get around to it." She shook her head at the Girlz. "I can't tell you how disappointed I am in you."

"But they came forward now!" Lily said. "And my punishment's all over, and my groundation at home. It doesn't matter anymore!"

"You got grounded too?" Zooey said.

"Wouldn't you have been?" Reni said. "My parents would have sent me to my room until I was sixteen if I—"

She stopped. Ms. Gooch's eyebrows did a short twitching thing.

"I think I'm beginning to understand this a little better," she said. "But, Reni, fear shouldn't have kept you from standing by your friend."

"I wanted to!" Reni said.

"She did," Zooey said, nodding as if her neck were on a spring. "She was all crying every day. Then we started to fight all the time—"

"Zooey, hush up," Reni said.

Suzy patted Zooey's arm.

"You see?" Kresha said. "It's okay!"

"It *will* be," Ms. Gooch said, "after you four take a little walk with me down to the office."

Four faces froze like cubes in an ice tray.

"Why?" Lily said.

"Because it's only fair that they get the same punishment you did—perhaps even worse—since they let you take the rap all by yourself."

Suzy burst into tears. Zooey breathed so hard, her face turned bright red. Kresha just looked confused, even as she muttered, "But it's okay. It's okay."

Only Reni squared her little shoulders and tilted up her chin and said, "Okay. We deserve it. I'm ready."

"Can I go too?" Lily said.

"No," Ms. Gooch said. "I don't want any bleeding hearts down there. It's time these girls faced up to their own mistakes."

Lily felt as if she were going to lose her Cheerios right there. "Could you tell Mr. Ronald one thing for me?" she said.

"What?" Ms. Gooch said impatiently.

"Could you tell him that they're good girls—that we just got carried away and we'll never do it again? And tell him—"

"Just a minute, Lily, let me get a notepad," Ms. Gooch. She shot her eyebrows up. "I'll make sure he knows, all right? Go on inside."

The time between then and first recess was the longest slice of school Lily had ever lived through. The Girlz didn't get back to class until just before the bell rang, and except for seeing that Suzy and Zooey had probably been crying nonstop the entire time, Lily couldn't detect any clues as to what had happened. One thing was nice though. At least she could look at them again—and they looked back.

The minute the bell rang, she bolted for the door, practically knocking Yale down in the process.

"Excuse me," she said.

"I got something," he said.

"We got all our stuff done already, Yale. We turned it in, remember?"

"No—" Yale swallowed, and for a second Lily was sure he was going to pull out his inhaler. "No, I got something for you," he said finally.

Out of the corner of her eye, Lily could see the Girlz waiting outside the door.

"Okay," Lily said. "So—are you going to give it to me?"

She was trying not to be rude, but the Girlz—it had been so long.

"Here," Yale said, and he gave her a piece of paper and ran.

Lily stuffed the paper into her pocket and darted out into the hall. The Girlz stood there, watching, waiting, and looking as sad as any four people Lily had ever seen. Even Kresha wasn't smiling.

"Are you guys all right?" Lily said. "You didn't get suspended, did you? That would be so unfair, because I didn't get suspended. I only had to stay after a week—*with* Shad Shifferdecker—but even that wasn't so bad because—"

"We didn't get suspended," Zooey said. "Or my mother really *would* kill me. As it is, she's taking away desserts for a month, and that's bad enough."

"They called your parents already?" Lily said.

"They made them come up here," Suzy said tearfully. "I never saw my father look like that before."

Lily's heart was racing. "Your parents didn't tell you that you couldn't be in the group anymore, did they?"

"No fun—one month," Kresha said.

The rest of them nodded, except Reni. She was just standing there, arms folded, twitching one foot.

"Girls, could we move this little discussion on out to the playground?" Ms. Gooch said behind them.

They hustled. There was no room for mistakes with this lady now.

Once they were out under their tree—which Lily almost hugged—she faced them all, the way she'd done dozens of times—the way she'd been afraid she never would again.

"I'm really sorry you guys got in trouble," she said to them. "Honest. I didn't want that. That wasn't why I left you that note."

"What note?" Reni said.

"The one I left in the clubhouse yesterday," Lily said.

"We haven't been to the clubhouse since day *before* yesterday," Suzy said.

"Yeah, we had this great big fight," Zooey said.

"Lot of screaming," Kresha said.

"We needed you to calm us down," Suzy said.

"That wasn't it."

They all looked at Reni.

"It was because we hated what we did," she said. "That's why we were acting all evil."

"And we thought you hated us," Suzy said. "Until yesterday when Kresha heard you talking to Shad and those guys."

"She said you wouldn't tell them it was us even though we knew Yale musta told you." Zooey's eyes grew round. "You were so brave, Lily. I could never be that brave—"

"You were all brave to tell on yourselves," Lily said. "I only got in trouble for the glue thing because I got caught!"

"I'm serious though," Reni said. "If we still want to have a club—"

"Yes!" Lily said. "Don't we?"

Heads bobbed.

"But we can't meet for, like, a month," Reni said. "My parents are so mad at me—I'm gonna be grounded 'til I'm old enough to drive."

"That's why you couldn't tell on yourself, huh?" Lily said. "Because your parents are so strict."

"Ve vait *too* long," Kresha said, wagging her finger.

"'Vait'?" Zooey said.

Lily threw back her head and laughed out loud. "I don't care how long we have to 'vait,' you guys, as long as we talk to each other and hang out at school. And we'll be so good, we'll never get in trouble like this again."

"Is that another step?" Zooey said.

"Should I write it down?" Suzy said.

Lily shook her head. "It takes the place of all the other steps."

"Good," Zooey said. "Those were too hard to remember."

"This is easy," Lily said. "First, you love God with everything in you. Got that?"

Again, heads bobbed.

"Then you love your neighbor the way you want to be loved."

"What happened to self-image?" Reni said.

"I think—but I'm not sure yet," Lily said, "—that if you're busy thinking about your image of other people and making room for God inside you, you'll end up liking yourself, like, automatically."

"Vhat?" Kresha said.

"You'll get it," Suzy said, patting her arm.

"We will?" Zooey said. "Are you sure?"

Suzy was still reassuring her when the bell rang. Kresha joined in with a chorus of "It's okay, Zo-wee. It's okay," as the three of them started off across the playground.

Reni hung back and slipped her arm through Lily's.

"I was so afraid you were gonna hate me forever," she said.

"You're my best friend!"

"I thought Yale was your new best friend."

"A boy?" Lily said. "I don't *think* so!"

"You still hate boys?"

Lily thought about it, and then she had to shake her head. "Not so much," she said. "My image of them has changed. Speaking of Yale," Lily said, digging in her pocket, "he gave me something."

"What is it?"

What it was, was a drawing—a Yale special—of Lily in a toga, complete with leaves in her hair. She smiled when she saw that she didn't look *that* ugly, at least not to Yale.

But it was what he had written at the bottom that really made her grin:
Thank yo fr beeng so nis to me.

It did more than make her grin. It made her feel pretty good about herself.

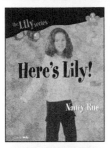

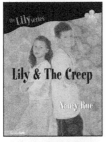

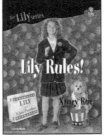

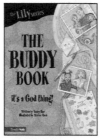

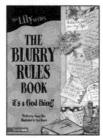

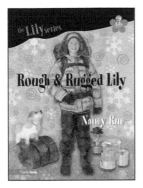
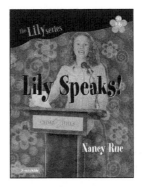

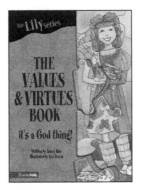